The Masters Review
ten stories

Volume III

Drew Ciccolo · Amanda Pauley · Eric Howerton
Maya Perez · Shane R. Collins
Courtney Kersten · Meng Jin · Joe Worthen
Andrew MacDonald · Diana Xin

Stories Selected by Lev Grossman
Edited by Kim Winternheimer and Sadye Teiser

Editor's Note

I am so pleased to share with you our anthology, *The Masters Review*, with stories selected by Lev Grossman for its third volume.

The goal of this anthology is to showcase writers in graduate-level creative writing programs. Our feeling, after reviewing submissions from programs around the world, is that these writers are among the best. We believe the stories you read here represent the start of ten bright careers and that these writers will continue to produce great work.

MFA, MA, and PhD creative writing programs are constantly under scrutiny, but the MFA debate seemed particularly heated this year. I am especially proud to be publishing these stories within the context of that debate. I feel *The Masters Review* makes a strong statement about the kinds of writers these schools produce, and I am happy to support any program that inspires the kind of beautiful writing you see here.

Each year we pair with a guest judge to help us select stories. For our past two collections, judges Lauren Groff and AM Homes chose pieces by authors who continue to astound us. *The Masters Review* authors have gone on to publish their first novels and short story collections. Our authors include a Nelson Algren Award finalist, an Academy of American Poets Prize winner, Fulbright Fellows, and our writers continue to publish in reputable literary journals across the country. We consider the authors in this collection to be part of the community of emerging writers for whom *The Masters Review* serves as a platform and a resource. In addition to publishing our printed anthology, *The Masters Review* works year-round to provide content for and by emerging writers. We're thrilled to add these new voices to our growing library.

For this collection we worked with *New York Times* bestselling author and *Time* book critic Lev Grossman. Mr. Grossman brings a wonderful balance to this collection. He is considered one of the best literary critics in the field, and he sees the magic in storytelling. It was an incomparable pleasure working with him, and our anthology is all the better because of his participation and perspective.

In our collection's opening story "The Behemoth," a giant falls from the sky. In "Go Down, Diller," a single father grapples with raising his daughter and understanding the bear who works at the burger joint down the street. "OpFor" is a story about a soldier departing for war, and "Braids" examines the intense and complicated microclimate of a prison hair salon. In "A Language Translatable by No One" Courtney Kersten writes a heart-wrenching essay about losing her mother, and in "Custody" a divorced mother tries to bond with her son on an African safari.

The stories in this collection are diverse, but each one carries an emotional truth. It is my feeling they are pieces of fiction and nonfiction that are impossible to walk away from unchanged. They are memorable and important. I hope you enjoy reading our third volume as much as we enjoyed preparing it for you, and I hope you find a voice in these pages that belongs to a writer you will continue to follow for years to come.

Kim Winternheimer
Founding Editor

The Masters Review

The Masters Review, Volume III
Stories Selected by Lev Grossman
Edited by Kim Winternheimer and Sadye Teiser

Front cover: istock photo gallery

Interior design by Mackenzie Griffith
www.mgbookdesign.com

First printing.

ISBN: 978-0-9853407-2-8

© 2014 The Masters Review. Published annually by The Masters Review. All rights reserved. No part of this publication may be reproduced or reprinted without prior written permission of The Masters Review. To contact an author regarding rights and reprint permissions please contact The Masters Review. www.mastersreview.com

Printed in the USA

Contents

The Behemoth • *1*

Braids • *11*

Go Down, Diller • *27*

Custody • *41*

OpFor (Oppositional Force) • *59*

A Language Translatable by No One • *65*

Electronic Heads • *75*

County Maps • *89*

The Turk • *97*

Someone Else • *109*

Introduction

I never went to an MFA program for the simple reason that I never got into one. I applied to half a dozen of them in the fall of 1991, and in the spring of 1992 I got back five rejections—and one waitlist, at Johns Hopkins, which if we're being honest we can probably chalk up to the fact that my father was a professor in the English department there at the time. Either way, I never made it off that waiting list.

I didn't get in because my writing wasn't good enough. I can't find the piece I used as my writing sample, thank God, but I remember it well enough to know that it was showy, arch, effortful, experimental, painfully self-conscious and weird-to-no-purpose. It was written by someone who was obviously deeply unclear on how you were supposed to go about gathering power into words. I would contrast it starkly with a story like Drew Ciccolo's "The Behemoth," of which this is the first line:

> A giant person fell out of the sky.

Seven words in and the spell has already begun: you can feel the tension, between the simple, calm declarativeness of the language and the deep strangeness of the meaning within it. You could power a small city with that tension.

Or look at the crisp simplicity of the opening of Shane Collins's "OpFor (Oppositional Force)":

> Cadet Warren Buehler gathered kindling—dried moss,

rotting sticks, some dead leaves—and arranged them into the shape of a teepee like he'd seen on survival shows.

Watch what he does: he grounds you in the sharp, high-def specificity of the kindling, then with the reference to survival shows he reaches out into the ether for cultural context. It's a sentence that goes from tweeter to woofer in thirty words.

If, in 1991, someone had been foolish enough to ask me what I thought literature would look like in 2014, this is not the book I would have described. I would have imagined something wild and experimental and illegible and possibly interactive. By those standards these stories are relatively tame. They're not shattered or inverted or deconstructed. Probably the most "experimental" of them—the aforementioned "The Behemoth"—owes its greatest debt to Donald Barthelme, a writer who died in 1989.

In other words these aren't stories about stories, these are stories, full stop. They're more interested in the world around them than they are in themselves. There's a hungry curiosity in them, a wealth of experience that seems to want to reach out and pull everything into it: a barbershop in a prison (Amanda Pauley's "Braids"), a safari in Namibia (Maya Perez's "Custody"), a delivery room in a Beijing hospital (Meng Jin's "Electronic Heads"), a chess tournament in a café in Paris at the beginning of the 19th Century (Andrew MacDonald's "The Turk").

They're frightening, funny, sexy, restless, strange and frequently melancholy, in the way short stories are. What they have in common is that they do what good writing has always done, and will always do, which is to console. There's a great line in Courtney Kersten's "A Language Translatable by No One" that's meant to apply to a piece of rhubarb pie, but it's equally true of any of these stories: "So, nothing can, you know, fix this, but, you wanna know fuckin' what? This shit, *this* shit, at least, you know, temporarily fixes it." In this world, that's as good as stories get.

Lev Grossman

The Masters Review
ten stories

The Behemoth

Drew Ciccolo
Rutgers–Newark University; MFA

A giant person fell out of the sky. That's the best we can explain it. This giant person landed smack dab in the middle of Mercy Park, our city's biggest and most beautiful public space. Mercy Park is closed, of course, from ten p.m. to five a.m. The behemoth landed at three a.m. on a Sunday, so no one, we think, was killed. If they were, they'd paid a dear price for violating a simple city ordinance.

The arrival sounded something like a hundred thousand orchestral bass drums booming in unison—one violent, echoing blast that shook the entire city. Even the deepest sleepers among us were startled awake. We stared at our ceilings or walls, our ears ringing, and thought, What in the F?

"What the F was that?" Lovers asked each other, their faces contorted in confusion. "What in the F'ing F?"

Our pets skittered across floors, taking refuge in the nearest closet. Our children appeared in our bedroom doorways, sucking their thumbs, tugging at their underwear, fresh tears spilling down their cheeks. Windows lit up all over the city. Sirens bayed up and down the streets. We hastily powered up our televisions, computers, and cell phones. Coffee pots percolated.

The first images were cryptic due to lack of light. We sat at our tables and sipped our coffee and stared at our screens, occasionally reaching out to pet our children's heads reassuringly. We saw vast stretches of oblong whiteness through air thick with mist. A spotlight swung over a pale, gigantic ear, which looked to some of us like a fetus coiled in utero. Those of us nursing hangovers quickly added a shot of brandy to our coffee. Some of us added double shots.

Reports began to appear: a massive person had fallen on Mercy Park, and the person seemed to be alive. We looked at each other in bewildered silence. Our newspeople reflected the stupefaction of our citizens, occasionally falling into silence themselves. The phrase "We don't know" such and such, the details, the being's origin, etcetera, emerged as a media refrain that would continue through the coming days and weeks. We couldn't blame them. We didn't know either.

Media outlets positioned television crews on high-rise rooftops. We watched in horror as the dawn light illuminated the giant person, who was completely nude, laying in our park. Mercy Park is a huge rectangle. It stretches from Calavera Street all the way up to Elle Street, quite a distance. Some of our city's finest buildings, including our tallest skyscraper, the Pinn Warnott Building, line the expanse of Mercy Park.

The behemoth took up the better part of the park. We watched its pale chest rise and fall in the overcast morning light. Microphones picked up the sound of its raspy breaths. Perhaps the most immediately distinct feature of the giant, aside from its size, was the lack of pigmentation in its skin and hair. Its half-closed eyes were an opaque grayish color and emanated an intense weariness. A broken cobweb of sparse, stringy yellow hairs hung from its scalp onto the discombobulated earth below. It had female-looking breasts with pink nipples, but its sex organ was abnormal. Only a pale nubbin of flesh poked out from between its legs. It was also missing a belly button. It looked alternately like a strange child and a very tired old person. We found it difficult to say. It had dark circles under its eyes and its lips were dry and cracked. This, along with the raspy breathing, the sheer size of its body, and its unhealthy-looking hair, made it seem old. The overall lack of body hair, the angelic lack of pigmentation, and the lack of any discernable wrinkles made it seem young. Either way, we decided, it was androgynous.

The entire scene, while surprising and remarkable, was decidedly dismal. It was one of those cloud-covered autumn mornings when the sky looks like it ends a hundred feet up in one infinite dirty gray quilt.

Our city is known for its beautiful park, with its many lawns, groves of trees, and elaborate gardens. Now it served as a bed for the behemoth.

Its heels were planted in Watchung Pond, which greatly disturbed the ducks, some of which could be seen perched in revolt on the tops of the behemoth's toes. Its head rested on a leafy grove of red oak, which had turned magenta that fall; the color provided a stark contrast to the pale, almost translucent face. The soft pines next to what used to be our tennis courts edged the left leg of the behemoth.

We placed calls to one another. Text messages shot across the city like airborne gremlins. Our phones buzzed or chirped their catchy dance numbers. What's happened? How can this be? Are we dreaming? Are these the end times? As far as we knew, there were no such things as giants. Were the disgruntled people passing out apocalypse flyers in our subway lobbies onto something? We had no precedent to cite. Some of us had heard of the little African man who had fallen on West London, but he was of relatively normal human size, and authorities had gathered that he was a stowaway on a jet plane, and fell when the landing gear lowered. No, there was no precedent.

"This is just . . ." we said into our phones, trailing off into baffled little utterances. "I mean it's just. . . ."

"It's horrible," we confirmed, locking ourselves in our bathrooms so our kids wouldn't hear. We couldn't help but harbor a strange excitement, however, somewhere in our chests. The behemoth, after all, was a visitor to our city.

We agreed to check in with each other when we knew more.

Our cats yawned on our windowsills. Our dogs looked at us expectantly, ready for their morning walks. Our children spooned cereal into their mouths. Our Sunday activities would have to be postponed. There would be no feigned singing from our pews at church, no visits to our seniors in their retirement centers, no shopping trips, no visits to the parks or playgrounds, no gym workouts.

We timidly poked our heads outside our windows and doors. Those of us who lived around the park were overwhelmed by the disturbing sound of the behemoth's wheezing breaths. At times the breaths grew frantic. At others they were slow and sporadic. Some of us said later that its breathing sounded like wind whistling through a colossal broken window. Aside from the breathing, an eerie silence had fallen over our city. We were at a loss.

We walked our dogs, in many cases neglecting to clean up their excrement due to our preoccupation with the behemoth. We exchanged worried looks with our neighbors. We raised our upturned palms. "Can you believe this shit?" our faces silently asked.

We were pleased that the behemoth had not fallen on us, but our stability was shaken. Would more giants fall? Would they land on our homes?

Much of the perimeter of Mercy Park was cordoned off with officers, police cars, and wooden police barricades. Announcements came over the news stating that we were not to leave the city. The government had put in place a citywide quarantine due to the unknown nature of the body. The quarantine inspired familiar anti-government sentiment within many. Our city is not the richest, and government aid has proven hard to come by. Now they were limiting our travel plans.

Would the behemoth speak to us? We certainly wanted an explanation. Soon our mayor was given a megaphone and raised up on a hydraulic crane attached to an electrical truck. The mayor had recently misallocated some city funds to pay for the breast augmentation surgery of an escort with whom he was involved; the scandal made quite the brouhaha. However, as we watched him standing alone in the dolly, megaphone in hand, we couldn't help but wish him the best.

The worker operating the crane situated the mayor level with the giant's ear canal.

"Hello there!" he said through the megaphone.

It was hard to see, but some of us thought we detected sweat on the mayor's brow. People peered out of the many windows of the many buildings located around the perimeter of the body in the park. They later admitted they had been too scared to leave their offices and apartments.

The behemoth didn't respond to the mayor. It continued wheezing. We watched expectantly.

"Hello there, I say!" repeated the mayor.

It looked as though the behemoth's pale lips parted ever so slightly. Still, it didn't respond.

The mayor was eventually lowered back down to the ground.

News cameras captured a bottle bouncing off the behemoth's forehead. Someone had thrown it from a high window or a rooftop. The news stations replayed it, zooming in. It was definitely a bottle. It looked like a green beer bottle. It was thrown, we figured, by one of our young rowdies. The news anchors seemed disgusted and disappointed by this, and we shared their sentiment.

Morning became afternoon. We realized that the behemoth was sick: the labored breathing, the cracked lips, the almost-closed, baggy eyes, the lack of movement. We showered or bathed. We watered our houseplants. We made probiotic smoothies. We played with our confused children.

The more adventurous among us put on our scarves and went to Mercy Park for a closer look. We walked slowly, our faces stoic. There would be no strolls along the leafy autumnal corridors of our park in the foreseeable future. That much was certain.

Many of our city's homeless appeared more lively, as they, of course, didn't feel quite the same attachment to the status quo. They sat open-legged with their backs against the sides of our buildings or rolled their squeaky carts along the sidewalks. Some smiled at us.

"We got a giant in the park," they informed us as we walked past.

We nodded our heads in affirmation.

"Could be an alien," they said.

We frowned and nodded.

"Looks human, though," they said.

We shrugged.

"Doesn't even have any clothes."

We smiled perfunctorily, some of us even half-heartedly winked, and we hurried off toward Mercy Park. Soon a crowd had gathered. Some of the more belligerent among us screamed things like "Who are you!" or "Tell us your name!"

Due to the size of the park, our city's services didn't have the resources to secure the entire perimeter. Some of us snuck in. The behemoth's body rose high in the air. One man attempted to shimmy his way up a strand of the behemoth's pale yellow hair, but was quickly called down by a police officer. Some of us could be seen at the base of a buttock, or leaning against a gigantic limp finger, as a friend took our photo. Some gave the cameras a thumbs-up while others could bring themselves to do nothing but stand unsmiling in the shadow of the great pale mass. Some later said they could hear the deep thudding of the behemoth's heart.

Groups of young rowdies ran right up and poked the body with fingers or tree branches, then ran off so as not to be crushed should the behemoth decide to roll over or stretch. We noticed that the behemoth's hands and feet seemed to be turning bluish.

As night fell, one of our city's benevolent societies handed out white candles. The sky was still overcast, filled with bulbous clouds, which sometimes parted to reveal a bright orange moon. Those of us surrounding the behemoth held a candlelight vigil. Its breaths were becoming fainter, more sporadic, the wheezing more of a rattle.

One of our city's most highly-praised entertainers, a young man called Smiley Edwards, was petitioned by the mayor and others to sing to the behemoth as a show of our good will. A stage on a flatbed truck was wheeled into Foley Field, which lay above the behemoth's head. We were all familiar with the soft rock recordings of Smiley Edwards, and his presence cheered us up.

Smiley's pianist tapped out the first few unmistakable chords of his most recent hit song, "Just Smile."

"I'm gonna need y'all to help me out on this one," Smiley said through his microphone. "I can't do this alone."

Then he began: "We, all of us, need a friend. . . ."

We joined in, hesitantly at first, gripping our candles and peering sidelong at each other. Soon, though, our voices rose into a spectacular chorus with Smiley's lovely tenor at the forefront. By the time we got to, "When the rain is coming down, just smile . . . when there's no one else around, just smile," our singing had become impassioned, even feverish. Our children felt it, too, and many of them began to harmonize and dance spastically at our feet.

During the instrumental section toward the end of the song, while Smiley pranced back and forth across the stage, a flight of doves was released into the air. Those of us watching from home, or lucky enough to have a clear view of the stage, later said they had never seen Smiley's face so emotional, and that tears welled in his eyes as he belted out, "Because the smile you give to me, may be the last I'll ever see," drawing out the last "see" longer than any singer had ever dared attempt to sustain a note.

At the end of the song, Smiley sank to his knees. He'd given it all he had. Overcome with emotion, we hugged each other. We nodded and patted one another on the back, our jaws clenched from the intensity of the thing.

We began to understand, at this point, that the behemoth was no longer breathing. It lay there completely motionless. Its chest had stopped rising and falling.

We stared with watery, confused eyes. The flames of our candles were by now getting low. News traveled: the behemoth, barring a miracle, was indeed dead. Many of the doves had landed on the behemoth. Some pecked at its eyes.

We were sad, tired, and confused. The wind picked up and drops of cold rain began to fall. Soon we retreated to our apartments or townhouses. We turned on our lights and stared at our hallways or kitchens or living rooms. Most of us made tea, be it herbal, oolong, black, white, or green, and sat together in silence. We received phone calls. Schools were closed the next morning.

"Of course," we said.

If the behemoth had caused a strange quiet when it was alive, this quietude was exacerbated even further by its death. We slept in starts and stops that night, if at all. We listened to the rain fall against our windows and roofs. Our children crawled into bed with us and we pulled the covers tight over their small bodies.

In the morning, we moped. Our choral rendition of "Just Smile" was replayed on our television screens, which caused us some embarrassment. The rain had stopped and the behemoth's body lay there wet and dead for all to see. A puddle of rainwater had formed in the concave dip of its belly-buttonless abdomen. Smaller puddles had also formed in the sockets of the behemoth's closed eyes.

We walked to Mercy Park to pay our respects. Many among us chose to wear dark clothing.

Various birds, mostly pigeons, had landed on the behemoth's body. Religious leaders from our city's churches, synagogues, mosques, and Buddhist temples led us in prayer at various locations around the body. Many of them failed to mask their confusion over what the behemoth might mean with regard to their religious doctrines, yet they led us in prayer nonetheless. The body looked even sicklier now that it was dead, as blood began to well underneath its skin. Its countenance radiated a peace we had never before seen. Although it was only with us for a day, the fact of its death shocked us. Its all-encompassing silence created within us an unusual stillness.

Street vendors set up stands selling t-shirts with photos or artists' renditions of the behemoth, over words like: "I Survived the Behemoth, What Else Ya Got?" or "Don't be Squeamish: It's Only the Behemoth" or "I Partied with the Behemoth." One of our more sensitive entrepreneur's shirts read: "R.I.P. The Behemoth–Never Forgotten." Perhaps shamefully, or not knowing what else to do, many of us bought the overpriced shirts.

The sun, a humongous ball of fire the size of 1.3 million earths capable of producing solar winds, flares, and firestorms, broke through in the afternoon. Workers were busy stretching industrial-sized tarpaulins, normally used on barges and landfills, over the behemoth's body. Did our city's brass think this was an acceptable solution? It seemed akin to quelling a gambling problem by drinking to excess. The mayor maintained that the behemoth's body was too large to move. Cutting it apart would be too ghastly, and perhaps too dangerous.

Our scientists and doctors gave interviews defending the covering of the body, explaining that the bacteria in the behemoth's intestine, assuming it had an intestine, had surely begun digesting the intestine itself, and would now begin digesting the surrounding internal organs. Flies would be attracted to the body and, if they hadn't already, lay eggs inside it. The bacteria would then break down tissues and cells, releasing fluids and gases. Maggots would move through it as a mass, spreading bacteria, secreting digestive enzymes, and tearing through tissue with their mouth hooks. The smells emanating from the body would attract blowflies, flesh flies, beetles, mites, and parasitoid wasps.

The bloated body would then blacken and collapse, the flesh turning viscous. The smell of decay would be overwhelming. The surface of the body in contact with the ground would mold as the body fermented. Beetles would succeed maggots as the primary consumers. The hair of the body, of which there wasn't much, would then slowly disappear, leaving only the behemoth's bones. This, they said, could take fifty days or a year, depending on factors such as the weather and the size of the local beetle and fly populations.

The prospect turned our stomachs, we had to admit, but there was something that disturbed us about covering the body. Many of us continued to gather around the behemoth, half-covered as it was with dark green and brown tarpaulins, but we'd lost our sense of purpose, however nebulous it had been.

Some of us went to the gym. The Pinn Warnott building contains a large gym on the eighty-third floor. Those of us who were members found ourselves on treadmills or stair-climbers, looking out through the window at the behemoth's corpse. Officials had run out of tarps and had only been able to cover parts of its legs and abdomen. It was a depressing sight, to say the least, and many of us cut short our workouts, telling ourselves we had all winter to get our bodies in shape for spring.

Those of us with elderly parents or relatives went to visit them. We looked through doorways as we walked down smooth hallways of hospitals and nursing homes, looking into the various rooms. We marked the stockinged feet sticking out from under flannel blankets, the occasional moans, or even bursts of cursing. Oftentimes one sock would be oddly disheveled or about to fall off. This sock, we thought, hung there stupidly, and it filled us with sadness and rage.

We peeked in at the faces of the bedridden. They gazed back at us, unimpressed, or dozed uncomfortably. We noticed their trays, their plates holding untouched brown meat, the potatoes and vegetables picked at ever so gingerly, the tiny cartons of milk still almost full, the cups of sherbet licked clean or left to melt.

When we arrived at the rooms of our loved ones, the ones we had come to visit, we strode in and leaned over them, kissing their foreheads and cheeks. We held their upper arms gently with our hands, feeling the meager warmth of their bodies, telling them we loved them and not wanting them to ever leave us.

Braids

Amanda Pauley
Hollins University; MFA

Two guards orchestrated the unlocking of doors and supply boxes. Each boxed section had a color-coded backing where the tools were hung—green behind clippers, red behind scissors, blue behind combs—so that it was evident which items were already out. Graydon and the other inmates, all in spotless khaki uniforms, moved toward their respective chairs. This was Graydon's second time on the inside. After making it through the training program, he had been a prison barber for five years during his last seven-year sentence at Jackson. Now being new to Taylorsville State Prison, he was working on a probationary period. Not only did he have to prove reliable to the supervisor of the work program, he had to prove that a six-foot, four-inch, pasty white guy with red hair and light-blue eyes could cut hair worth a damn, no matter the race or ethnicity of the head it grew on. He had been in for only five weeks this time, and inmates already tried to bargain with the more flexible guards to get the right place in line to land in his chair.

"We got seven guys coming from orientation at ten. Work on the others until they get here," the guard said.

Graydon heard the barber two chairs down say exactly what he thought. *Shit.* For the most part, Graydon liked his job. Barbering had advantages over working in the cafeteria, machine shop, or janitorial services. The barbers were a mainstay for prisoner communication, and they earned tips in the form of packets of mackerel or tuna, postage stamps, or X-rated magazines, cigarettes having died out with the smoking ban. But Graydon hated doing the new guys, who sometimes had a wealth of hair. According to policy most of it had to go. Some of them hated losing their dreads and braids or long bushy beards more than anything else about the transition to the inside, except for leaving their families, and it was the barbers who took off their hair.

One guard stayed with the barbers. The other went out in the hall, where two more guards waited with a line of inmates.

"One, six, four, seven, three, three, two. Come on up. Far chair."

"One, six, five, three, nine, eight, one." The guard called numbers until all five chairs were occupied.

The barbers made twenty cents an hour. Graydon thought that was ludicrous. Sad too, when he considered how much he made selling weed over the course of a few hours when he was out.

"What's up Thompson?" This was the second time that Thompson had ended up in Graydon's chair, and that was no accident. Graydon put a cape around his neck and remembered that Thompson liked his big white head mostly shaved, with a little length left over his flat spot to even things out.

"Block 12 is betting on that big lady guard's weight." Thompson laughed.

"Shit, she gotta be three-hundred," Graydon said, reaching for the clippers. "How the hell they gonna verify that?"

"After you get your ass out from under her, you gonna tell us. That's how." Thompson's eyes were closed, his face smiling.

"You think so? If I get under that and live to get out, I ain't telling nobody."

Graydon looked to see how far away the guard stood. Down the line at chair five, the guard was busy looking at the foot pump on a chair that wasn't working. Graydon pretended to adjust the clippers in his hands and asked, in a low voice, "Who's taking bets for the game this weekend?"

"Dwight is. Hey, do my hair like you did last time, all right. But do me a chin strap."

"You know I can't. You leave this chair with facial hair and you'll be right back here with my ass on the line." Graydon's leg bumped Thompson's arm as he turned the chair into position. Thompson winced.

"What's up with your arm?"

"Derek did a tattoo for me last night." Thompson kept his voice low under the white noise of the shop.

"I thought he quit. He fucked that one guy's arm up bad."

"Naw, I saw the last three he done. All came out fine."

"I'd keep an eye on that thing. You're going to wake up with your arm rotting off."

"I think something else went down with Miller's arm. You ought to get a tattoo while he got enough chess pieces saved up to melt down."

Thompson was no small man, but Graydon still had to pump the chair up four times to get it to where he didn't have to bend over. The sound of Graydon's clippers joined the others and he went to work on Thompson's flat spot. He was leaning in close to Thompson's face and could see Thompson wanted to say something else so he stopped the clippers and pretended to inspect his hairline.

"We need a fourth to go in on a bag of juice." Thompson spoke quietly.

"Who made it?"

"That tall mother fucker that says he's Amish. The electrician. Nathan, I think."

"How many mackerels I have to trade?"

"Ten each. It should be good. Deryll saw it. He paid Deryll to check on the bag a couple of times. Let the air out of it. He's got it in one of the washers. Been sitting for twelve days. He used sugar and strawberries Lewis got working in the kitchen."

"That's a lot of mackerel."

"Well, you do this haircut as good as you did before and I'll see you two out in the yard later."

"You know they ran some of us past a breathalyzer in the lunch line last week."

"Well, don't eat lunch that day, shithead." Thompson smiled.

Thompson was one of three guys Graydon almost trusted. "All right, I'm in." Graydon finished Thompson, two more guys, and was working on Chew.

"New guys coming in after you finish with him," the guard said.

Chew had a beautiful round black head. With one more run of the clipper it was completely bald.

"Looks good, looks good! You a'right for a white man. Don't you worry about what anybody says," Chew said. Graydon smiled and uncaped him. "Newbies coming huh? Hee! Fresh meat for the punks." He winked at Graydon. "I'll catch you in the yard later."

Graydon nodded. Chew's personality cycled dramatically and

Graydon was pretty sure he was under the effects of some recently acquired hydrocodone. Graydon gave his space a quick sweep with the broom and calculated how much he had in tips so far today. Eight packets of mackerel, and it was early yet. With the six he already had in his locker he'd have plenty for getting in on the juice.

Graydon had just cleaned up his station when the fresh meat, as Chew put it, came around the corner. His heart dropped at the sight of the longest, thickest, black braids he had ever seen. They almost reached the back of the guy's knees, and the guy looked out of some angry blue eyes. He was not as tall as Graydon, but he was built like a truck. Tattoos ran out of his short-sleeved uniform and down the brown skin of his arms. One forearm said: *Trust No One!* The numbers just above his knuckles put him in a gang out of Tidewater. A snake image twisted up out of his collar and around his neck with the head just below his cheekbone. The snake's tongue was out and flicked at the bottom of his earlobe.

Graydon held his breath. Back in Jackson, Graydon had been the end of a guy's fifteen-year-old dreads. The prison required it, not Graydon, but he had had the shit beat out of him in the yard later. That had prompted his beating the shit out of two other guys to get some of his reputation back. He'd spent four weeks in the hole for that.

The guard motioned for the guy to take Graydon's chair. He sat down without a word and looked at Graydon in the mirror.

Two hundred miles away Graydon's wife's head was bent over her own client. The man's head was all the way back, and Julie was thankful that his eyes were closed. He was not a particular favorite of hers. His breath was stale and she cringed even as she massaged his scalp, knowing how much he liked it. Julie was twenty-seven, and this guy was at least fifty, but he was a regular and an excellent tipper. She stretched her neck to one side and then the other, tired from doing three colors and four cuts already. The apple shampoo smell almost blotted out the perm smell coming from Ashley's client three chairs down the line. The shampoo girl had called in sick, so the hairdressers were doing their own washes. Julie rinsed and then ran her hands over her client's head to remove the excess water. She could tell without looking directly at his face that he had opened his eyes and was watching her chest as she worked. She blotted his head with a towel and left it hanging over his face as he sat up. "Okay, you can head on over to my chair."

He lifted the corner of the towel up and looked out at her. "You don't seem yourself today," he said.

"Just tired. Graydon went back in last month."

Her client sat down in the chair and she put her foot on the lever. Julie stood five feet two inches tall, and with one pump they were already eye to eye.

"Sorry to hear that. I didn't know he was going back," he said, looking more hopeful than sorry.

Her station was diagonal to Ashley's, and she saw Ashley give her a look in the mirror and roll her eyes.

"Yeah, well." She left it at that. She was grateful that he let her work in silence for a minute. A hairdresser's day was endless talking. Lately, she preferred the quiet ones, the eyes-closed-let-me-rest ones. When Graydon went back in, she had considered not telling anyone, but there was no doubt word would get out. So she told all of the girls at the shop and most of her clients since most of them knew everything about her personal life anyway. There had been plenty of sympathy. Only a few looked down their noses at her for sticking with a small-time, red-haired, drug-dealing giant, who couldn't keep himself out of prison even for the sake of his wife and child. It wasn't like he tried to kill anyone. This time. It had been marijuana and Joel's coke. At least Graydon swore to her that it was Joel's coke.

She finished and handed her client a mirror to check out the back.

"Looks great," he said.

"Glad you like it. I'll meet you out at the counter."

Usually she let the receptionist ring people up, but she had begun walking them to the front and doing it herself. Julie had discovered that clients tipped better since Graydon's return to prison, so she made the extra effort to see them out. This guy handed her a substantial tip, but he grasped her hand and held on. Julie's stomach turned, but until the transaction was over, she kept her feelings from surfacing.

"If you want some company, just call me." He winked at her and finally let go.

"Thanks." Julie forced a smile.

Ashley had come up behind her pretending to look for something. "Get that creep out of here," she whispered to Julie as he went out the door. "God, he's such a sleaze."

"Yeah, but the more cleavage I show, the bigger his tip." She opened her hand to show Ashley the wad of cash.

"Holy . . ." Ashley whispered.

While Julie cleaned her station, Ashley continued to make fun of the guy, until several ladies in the chairs were laughing. Linda, the owner, raised her eyebrows and Ashley quit, but even Julie was hard put to stop laughing. She needed to laugh, and Ashley, with her baby face and dyed-blonde hair down to her waist, could get her there every time. Ashley had been her best friend since they were kids and they had shared everything. When Julie was sixteen, and her grandmother had asked her for a life-altering favor, Ashley had helped write the letters.

Julie's next client was installed in her chair and talking a steady stream, but Julie was only half-listening. She nodded and smiled while she used a curling iron to cook large ringlets back into the straightened black hair, but she was thinking about those letters.

"Julie, I want you to do something for me," her grandmother had said.

Julie and Ashley, both wearing tank tops and short shorts, were painting each others' toe nails on the steps behind her mother's trailer. A copy of *Vogue*, rescued from the neighbor's trash, was open beside them. Julie's father was long gone, and her mother, Eileen, was out with her latest boyfriend. Julie's grandmother pulled up in the drive and got out. Her grandmother was a Holy Roller, the opposite of Eileen. Julie remembered her grandmother standing in the yard watching them. Her elderly skin was almost a translucent white, peppered with brown spots.

"There is the nicest boy. His name's Graydon, and he goes to church with his mamma every Sunday. He was the best-behaved child. He's nineteen now, and he got himself in a little trouble. They've sent him off to state prison. He really shouldn't be in that place. He's in with killers and all sorts. His mother has gone to pieces. I've written to him a couple of times, but I think it would help him if someone young were to write him a letter. Just a short note to say: How are you? I hope you're doing okay. Something to let him know he's not forgotten."

"What'd he do?" Ashley asked.

"A silly thing," Her grandmother said. "He messed up someone's car when he got mad at them."

"Oh." Ashley looked disappointed.

"Okay," Julie agreed. "I guess I can. Maybe a short letter." She tried to look casual about it, but the idea of a prison penpal was thrilling.

After her grandmother left, Julie convinced Ashley it would be an adventure of sorts. Ashley made suggestions while Julie wrote. Julie signed her name as loopy and grand as possible. To give Ashley some credit, she let her sign, *Hi from Ashley*, in the margin. They dropped the letter off directly at the post office. Julie's grandmother never saw the contents.

The first letter was simple. His reply was less brief. Within a matter of months, Julie and Graydon knew everything there was to know about each other. Julie read each letter to Ashley, and Ashley always had a hand in the response. Julie's grandmother's description of Graydon's prison charge had been slightly contorted. He had "messed up someone's car" indeed, when he fired a pistol at his ex-girlfriend as she drove her car away, after he discovered that she had cheated on him. Attempted murder was the official conviction. After Julie turned eighteen, she had filled out the visitor application form as Graydon suggested, writing *friend of the family* under the acquaintanceship question.

That visit, and the ones that followed over the years, were more electrically charged than an American Electric Power Plant. Inmates and their visitors were only allowed an embrace, a peck on the cheek, and then a goodbye hug, with no touching in between. Graydon and Julie mostly sat and stared at one another in a quiet heat. Graydon was obviously attracted to the slightly younger girl out of nowhere who wrote letters of lusty encouragement and described his future freedom, and parties, and him holding her, her legs wrapped around his tall waist while they danced around their own kitchen when they got married. Julie thought Graydon was not bad looking: his red hair unusual, his size incredible. Their relationship was taboo and romantic, but best of all, he was all hers, locked away and guarded from the world. He was her Rapunzel in a tower.

Julie didn't tell her grandmother what she was doing until after a couple of visits, but her grandmother, still remembering the sweet little boy she had seen in church, was not upset.

"He was such a quiet child," she said. "I'm sure he's learned from this." Her grandmother asked Julie if they shouldn't go visit him together.

"He's so lonely in there, Grandma. Wouldn't it be better if we went separately? That way he has twice as much to look forward to."

Julie dated other guys, slept with other guys, but she never quit writing and visiting Graydon. Whenever Eileen got a letter out of the mailbox, marked Jackson State Prison, Inmate # 66521-408, she shook her head and handed it to her daughter. "I don't know why on earth you keep writing to someone in prison."

"Grandma Anna asked me to. She felt sorry for him," Julie said.

"Well, I wouldn't feel for sorry for any man," Eileen said.

Her mother left for an evening shift of waitressing at the IHOP. Ashley came over, and Julie showed her the latest letter. This one had a photo of Graydon in it. He was standing in front of a plastic backdrop with a painting of the ocean and boats and palm trees. The backdrop was ripped at the bottom and curled upward, revealing the brick wall behind it. Graydon looked self-conscious in the photo.

"He's huge." Ashley giggled.

"He's really white," Julie said. "I've never been out with a guy with red hair."

"It's a wonder, with all the guys you've been out with," Ashley joked.

Julie looked at her hard. "You're right there with me, you know."

They were nineteen now, and Julie followed her mother's pattern and changed her mind about men on a monthly basis. Julie was not convinced that her mother was sure who her real father was.

"Graydon asked for a picture of me in a short skirt," Julie told Ashley one day.

"Are you going to send one?"

"I'd like to surprise him with something even better."

The two got a camera and went to work on nude photos.

"The one with just the sun hat is definitely the best," Ashley said.

The photo was returned with a notice from the Virginia Department of Corrections regarding the content. Nude photos were not allowed. Julie was remembering how she had posed in the photo with one hand on the hat, when she burned her client's forehead with the curling iron.

"Ow!" the lady screamed.

"I'm sorry! I'm so sorry!" she said.

"Ow! Ow! Ow!" The woman continued to shriek until Julie said she wouldn't charge her anything. She applied cream to the burn.

Fuck! She needed that money. She also needed to take Evan to see Graydon, but she was not sure she *wanted* to go. The lady left the shop with a small scar and no charge for the service, vowing never to come back.

By six o'clock Julie's chair was empty, Ashley's too. "Mom owes me a favor. She'll keep Evan tonight if we want to go out," Julie said.

Ashley smiled. "Come on, let's get a drink."

Since the guy in his chair didn't speak, Graydon did.

"How would you like it? They'll let me leave the braids down to your collar if you want, but I'm supposed to take all the facial hair off. Sorry." Graydon didn't like to apologize. He didn't make the rules, but he felt it necessary to show some sympathy. The guy's nostril's flared.

"Shit," was all he had to say.

Graydon didn't know what else to do but wait for an answer. A guard saw him not doing anything. "What's the hold up? We got a line out here. Cut his hair already."

Graydon looked from the guard back to the reflection of the blue-eyed man in his chair.

"Take it all. Cut them all fucking off. Wait . . ." The guy turned from the mirror to look directly at Graydon. "You cut a black man's hair before?"

"Yeah. I cut hair five years in Jackson State before here. Done hundreds of black guys. You want a skin fade or what?"

"Yeah. A skin fade." The guy faced the mirror again.

Graydon picked up the scissors, and took one of the braids in his hand. He looked in the mirror and noticed that all of the other guys had somebody in their chair, but none with the length of rope that he felt in his fingertips just then. Every eye in the room was on him. The braids were neat and smooth. He started to ask the guy how long he'd been growing his hair, but thought better of it. The braids fell to the floor like fat snakes. *Thwap! Thwap!* Graydon cut the hair as close to the guy's head as he could with scissors and then started with the clippers.

Somebody down the line was using hair oil. The smell reminded Graydon of the hair gel his wife used. He'd been in for five weeks, and Julie had only come to see him twice, bringing Evan, their son. Evan seemed to enjoy the noise of the visitation room. He laughed and played, if somewhat shyly, with the other kids. His mess of light-brown curly hair made him look like he'd always just gotten out of bed. Evan was three now, born a year after Graydon had gotten out the first time. They had not been married when Evan was born, but Graydon signed the paternity-acknowledgement form in the hospital. He knew there had been other men in Julie's life: Ty, Erick, Dale, maybe even some she hadn't told him about, but he was so caught up in the moment that he didn't care. Graydon and Julie had been on and off ever since his time in state prison ended four years ago. They got married two months after Evan was born, but their 'on and off's' continued.

Graydon wasn't sure what was going on with his wife now. He had expected her to come every Sunday, and he missed Evan terribly. Julie had been different at the first visit and more distant during the second. In fact, she had been a little strange ever since his weed sales had turned into a Felony for Possession of Cocaine with Intent to Distribute, and a two-year sentence because of Joel, the guy he was riding with, and because of the crack that was under Joel's seat. He told Julie he didn't know about that, which wasn't quite true.

Graydon felt lucky. Maybe that was not the right word, but after having done seven years, a two-year sentence seemed bearable. Those seven years came after he shot at his ex-girlfriend's car. The car. He shot at the *car*. But his ex-girlfriend and the other passengers said he was aiming at them, inside the car. He had wanted to blow her tire out, but he ended up with an Attempted Murder charge.

Now he had his white, freckled hands on this guy's head, trying to edge-up the hair line to perfection. Graydon kept a neutral expression, but he found it interesting that this medium-black-skinned guy had eyes as light blue as his own. Graydon looked all the way around the guy's head before he gave him a mirror to check out the back. Graydon had to admit, the guy had a good-looking head, and the cut was one of the best he'd ever done.

The guy looked in the mirror blankly, for what felt to Graydon like a long minute. Suddenly, the guy was grinning from ear to ear and nodding his head. Graydon stood still, waiting to see if he was headed for another shit-kicking competition or if the guy was a fruit loop.

"Not bad," the guy said.

Graydon looked around and noticed the rest of the new guys were gone. The others were working on regulars. He had taken quite some time on this guy.

"You done?" a guard asked.

Graydon nodded.

"Clifton, take this one back."

Graydon watched him leave with the guard. Maybe his hair hadn't meant that much to him. Or maybe he was aware that he looked pretty fucking good either way. Who knew? Over the afternoon, information passed through the barbershop. The guy's name was Hunter, he was in for first degree, and he already had some clout at Taylorsville. Getting on his good side wouldn't be a bad thing for Graydon's reputation or his tips. Now, if he could just figure out what was up with his wife.

Later, Graydon went to the showers in his flip-flops. He'd worn flip-flops in the shower for so long his first time in, that even when he got out he wore flip-flops in the shower. It drove Julie nuts. He smiled when he thought of the mad look on her face. She was cute. He checked his inmate email account as soon as he was done in the barbershop. There was an email from Julie. She was coming to see him the next weekend. He was relieved. That night he lay in his top bunk listening to the noises of the one hundred and forty-three guys who shared the dormitory, thankful that at least fat-ass Wilson in the bunk below him snored softly, and stunk only part of the time. And as he did so many times at night, he went over in his head the first time he was released from prison, and the fun that followed. Before things got bad.

Julie was twenty-three, and he was twenty-six. Graydon had been overwhelmed. He started to hyperventilate on the way to the car. She had made a point of looking particularly good that day. Julie could rock a short haircut. Graydon always told her she looked sweet, but street. From the minute they opened the door and he saw her standing outside, he had wanted to bite her, tear into her, and squeeze every part of that feminine little body, which came with an enormous set of implants, which she said her mother had paid for. He didn't buy that story, but he didn't press her on it either. They looked great. While it wasn't a first time for either one, it was *their* first time, and neither was disappointed.

They had driven to the nearest parking lot, a gas station next to a McDonalds, about five miles down the highway from the prison. Julie was driving but he was all over her, and neither could wait a minute longer. She barely had the Chevy in park and the engine off before he reached over and lowered the driver's seat, which never worked the same after the next thirty minutes. In plain view of the highway they screwed the daylights out of one another. Graydon had prepared himself the night before while he had a minute alone in the shower, hoping it would keep him from going too quickly the next day. He was working up to a second round, but Julie, who was on top by then, caught sight of a cop car. They drove further down the highway and pulled off at another exit to screw again as soon as Graydon was ready. A four-hour trip turned into an eight-hour ride of their lives. The trailer park fairy tale lasted for a year. Then Evan was born, the money got even tighter than before, and Graydon increased his drug sales.

Once a month, Julie's boss let the girls do each other's hair when things were slow, and didn't charge for supplies. Ashley had washed and cut

Julie's hair, and was about to apply color.

"Will it be bright red or deep red?" Julie asked.

"Just trust me. I saw a girl with this color last Friday night when we went to Four Flavors. She looked hot, and you have the same skin tone."

"Okay, go ahead." Julie closed her eyes and listened to the radio. The owner kept it on a station that played music from anywhere in the past fifty years. Oasis was holding one of the long notes in "Wonderwall" just then. Ashley sang along quietly, and Julie let herself relax.

Ashley was right. Her hair came out a deep, dark red, and it suited her. Julie was thrilled. She had never looked better when Dale came in the door asking for a cut. Dale was Evan's real father. At least she was pretty sure. Last Friday at the club, Dale had paid her considerable attention. He was smaller than Graydon and not nearly as much of a tough guy, but Dale was not locked up. He now had one of the most desirable qualities she could think of as she leaned over his face. The warm water darkened his curly brown hair. She massaged the shampoo in slowly. He watched her face, and she was not unhappy.

On Sunday, Julie stood in line outside the prison visitation room holding Evan's hand. He was four years old, and Julie could see this was an adventure to him, not unlike going to the grocery store. She was grateful she did not have to explain his father to Evan, Graydon *or* his real father. Evan never blinked when Julie said that Daddy had a new job in a different state. He smiled and said loudly to whoever would listen, *Daddy's working! He cuts hair like mommy.* Other women stood in line with the required see-through plastic bags containing their car keys, driver's licenses, and change for the vending machine. They smiled at Evan and then went back to adjusting their push-up bras and tight jeans while holding onto toddlers and readjusting babies in their arms. Julie remembered doing the same thing when she first visited Graydon back at Jackson, trying to look as good as regulations allowed when regulations stated: *Body must be covered. Underwear is required. Hems, slits or splits of dresses, skirts, shorts, etc., may not exceed four inches above mid-knee.*

Julie looked at the wives waiting to see their husbands, mothers hoping to see their sons, brothers hoping to see their brothers, and kids hoping to see vending machines. She knew the drill. *Where contact visiting is provided, handshaking, embracing, and kissing are ordinarily permitted within the bounds of good taste and only at the beginning and at the end of the visit.* Julie imagined the fuck fest that might take place if the guards weren't there. She watched as those already admitted waited for their own personal inmate to pop out of a far door. Some inmates had already emerged and were with their families at the vending machines. The inmates were not allowed to touch the money, so someone had to put it in the machine for them, and then they could pull out their Mountain Dew or Snickers or cold sandwich.

Julie's turn came. The guard took her driver's license and form, and then handed the license back to her. She went over to the waiting area while the guard paged Graydon. She listened to the conversations that filled the large bluish room full of plastic chairs. It was getting louder by the minute.

How are you? Fine, how are you? I miss you. How are the kids? Is everything going okay? I wish I could see Patrick. I miss going to the store. And falling asleep with you. I miss your sausage gravy, mom. I miss working at the shop with you, dad. I miss holding you, Amy. How's work? I miss going to that bar where they serve eggnog even in July. I had to spend three days in the hole after I kicked the shit out of that guy over there. We get to watch Criminal Minds, if we all agree on it. I wish I could be with you. I wish you had more money. I'm sorry that I only make $19.20 a month working in here. You got your hair cut. Looks sexy. What can I send you? Your love baby. Is the neighbor still complaining about the barking? Have you been down to the pond since we went? Did you drive straight here? How's he doing in school? Do the other kids give him a hard time about me being in here? Are you sorry you married me? No baby, never.

The angst and desperation of these conversations used to excite her, but now they gave her a headache. Graydon finally came out. Evan squealed and ran to him. Julie hugged him too, but with less enthusiasm. They sat down beside each other as they always did so they could hear one another. Evan sat in Graydon's lap and felt his father's face. Julie ran down the list of who said to say hi and how everyone was doing, but she had become mechanical.

"Evan, you want to run over to the play room and grab a toy?" Graydon pointed to the kids' area, which was full of parents with toddlers. Evan was off and running.

"Come right back," Julie said.

"Your hair looks great." Graydon smiled at her, hoping she had done it for him.

"Thanks." She gave a weak smile.

"What's going on with you?" Graydon asked. "I know we were fighting a lot before I left but you seem really different. Even more than the last time you came."

"Well of course I'm different. We're in a prison. It's not exactly *good times*. I'm not sure how you want me to act." She could tell this set him back. The change in her had surprised her too. It felt cold to say those things, but it was true.

"I don't want you to act. I want you to be yourself. Happy. Like before."

"Graydon, I can hardly pay the bills and keep Evan in day care. I'm tired."

"But not too tired to go out to the club. Isn't that what you said on the phone?"

"We just went that one night. I got to have some fun. All I do is work and take care of Evan."

She stopped talking as a guard went by. They watched as he walked on, up and down the rows of people. Julie saw a lady's hand go back in her pocket quickly as the guard went by. She wondered what the lady was going to give her man. Some gum? A photo? Pills? Julie looked around to see how close the lady was to a camera. Too close. *What an idiot.*

"Well did you?" he asked.

"Did I what?" she asked.

"Did you have fun? Did you get plowed?" he asked.

She raised an eyebrow. Evan returned and climbed on Graydon's lap with a blue plastic raccoon. The tail was missing.

"Plowed, drunk, not plowed, plowed. Well, either?"

"Plowed, plowed, Daddy?" asked Evan.

"Woah! Look whose listening." Graydon's voice softened.

"Look, Daddy, I got a raccoon. He looks like Blue," Evan said.

"He does? Who's Blue?" he asked.

"I got him a puppy. I was hoping it would help him not notice, you know, that a certain person was missing."

"Oh. Blue, huh? Blue's a good name." Graydon reached out and squeezed Evan's hand. "I love you, Little Man."

"I love you too, Daddy."

"Graydon . . ." she began, but he cut her off.

"He's mine," Graydon whispered toward her ear. "My name's on that paper, and he's mine."

"Graydon. What if . . . what if someone else could give him a better life?"

Graydon looked as if he had been stomach punched. "He's mine! God damn you. Mine! You said so yourself when he was born. He's mine!"

Graydon was yelling and pointing to his chest. His face was as red as his hair, and his eyes looked wet.

Evan started to cry. The entire room went silent, everyone looking at them. Julie took him from Graydon's lap. He let her.

"First and last warning," a guard said, pointing a finger at him.

The noise in the room started to build again. People lost interest and went back to their business except for a few more glances.

"Sorry, little man. Sorry. Daddy got upset. It's okay."

Evan's crying soon subsided.

"Julie, he's my son. I don't care how it . . . we, WE been raising him for three years."

"Well, now I'm raising him. And it's hard. And you said you had quit selling and you lied," Julie whispered.

"We needed the money for him." Graydon looked sick. "For us. I love you."

"Graydon, I loved you too, but . . ."

"Daddy," Evan interrupted.

"What Little Man?" Graydon reached over and held his hand. Evan still had tears in his eyes. His little fingers curled around Graydon's pointer finger.

"You work here?" Evan asked.

Graydon smiled. "Yes sir. I work here. I'm a barber. I cut people's hair. Like this." Graydon reached over and made the sound of a clipper while he ran his hand over Evan's head.

Evan giggled, and Julie bit her lip.

At three o'clock everyone stood up and started their goodbyes. Graydon hugged Evan and then Julie. Julie felt Graydon hang onto her long after she relaxed her hold, and almost long enough to get another guard's attention. She looked around at the others while Graydon told Evan goodbye again. Some were tearful, some looked thankful the time was up. Julie knew well the transition that took place for some between here and the parking lot. She could see it in their faces. The inmates stayed in the minds of some, like something stuck right up there, just to the left of the front of the brain, that never quite went away, day or night, while others were forgotten the minute their person got in the car and drove past the gate.

Graydon sat on the edge of his cot holding a photo of Evan, knowing that Julie had slept with someone. Probably Dale. Dale had been in and out of their lives for years, and he hated him. Julie had dated him before they got married, and now he was sure Dale had been on top of his wife, coaxing her to leave him, hoping that two years of separation would split them apart.

The only thing Graydon could do was go back to his bunk, or join a game of cards, then watch television and wait. He missed the free world, but out there things seemed to go wrong. The woman he wanted was there, the child he wanted was there, cars and sunsets, movement and freedom, everything was out *there*. The last time he was released, he went back to auto repairs because, on the outside, it didn't seem right somehow, doing the same kind of job his wife did. Not to mention, an auto repair shop was a prime location for selling drugs.

In here, he had a place, a role, even somewhat of a reputation. He was the best at something. He was pursued, even if it was by two-ton men with records who wanted their face shaved before hairs became ingrown. That was something. Graydon picked up a copy of the prison newsletter. It read: Get ready! Get ready for your release! Learn better communication skills. New recreational classes also starting this month. Sign up soon! *What, and learn to crochet? No mother fucker, no thank you.*

After lights out, Graydon sat on his top bunk, listening to the sounds of one hundred and forty-three men in various stages of sleep, snores and clogged sinuses, squeaky bunks, and the effects of dinner on so many intestinal tracks. He thought about the look on Hunter's face when he had finished cutting his hair and handed him the mirror. Right before he broke into that white-toothed, woman-getting grin his face had gone blank, his eyes glazed. It was like Hunter was falling, and then suddenly he latched onto something mid-air and pulled himself up into that smile. But what? Anger? A little bit of crazy? Graydon wasn't sure, but he had to find out.

Go Down, Diller

Eric Howerton
University of Houston; PhD

Diller McCaslin spent much of his morning famished and fast-forwarding through surveillance footage, hoping to catch the menace whose nightly mission it was to overturn the hotel's trash bins. Earlier that morning his daughter Shelly had missed the bus, causing him to forgo his own breakfast so he could safely deliver her to first period. When pulling out of the school's parking lot he saw a banner announcing the Fall Formal. He made a mental note to talk to Shelly about whether she planned on going and who with, though it would be some time before he remembered to ask about the dance.

When the bins finally toppled across the video screen, the culprit was nowhere to be found. The trashcans sat horribly askew, spilling soggy cardboard particles and creeping oozes, but the violator had avoided detection yet again.

Probably some damned animal, Diller thought.

At noon he locked the surveillance reels in the cabinet and headed to the parking lot. His stomach growled. As he made his way to his car, Diller spotted Wine Guy unloading a case from the back of a mid-1980s passenger van. "Wine Guy" was what Diller called the schmuck Snopes Vineyards had commissioned to pour wine at the hotel four days a week.

"Ducking out for a bite?" Wine Guy called to Diller. At the time he didn't know a cursory nod could be much of a mistake until Wine

Guy added, "Grab me a small something, yeah?" Diller was so taken aback by Wine Guy's forwardness—they'd never been friendly to one another—that in his confusion he'd agreed in a perfunctory way, if only to end the conversation quickly.

Now that he was next in line to order at Frontier! Burger, he wondered if it was too late to renege. He could apologize to Wine Guy, claiming he was so entrenched in his routine that he'd forgotten to pick up extra, though the last thing he wanted to do was apologize to someone who was still riding the coattails of his high school days by working a job that only required him to be cool and good looking. The man poured wine into little cups for crying out loud! Such people didn't deserve the moral sacrifice of a lie or the bending effort of an apology, and so Diller was left with no other choice but to buy him a burger.

When a voice low and murmuring finally slipped out the two-way speaker, Diller had only eighteen minutes left on his break.

"Well-established fontina purger, cannabis hell pew?"

Diller tilted his head to the side. "I'm sorry, I didn't catch that."

"Cunilingus tanker hoarder?"

Impatient to get the ball rolling, he said, "I'm having some trouble understanding you so I'm just going to go ahead?" Silence followed. He ordered and was relieved to find that each item dutifully appeared on the monitor nestled within the drive-thru menu.

"Inny ding elves?" the speaker crackled.

Intuitively, Diller said, "That's all."

"Thirst dwindle."

Pulling forward, he found the drive-thru window shut and tinted too dark to see through. He drummed the dash. When the window hinge squeaked open, a large, hairy paw emerged, rushing from the darkness toward him, clawing for money. Diller screamed, drowning out what sounded an awful lot like a dog barking numbers. Instinctively, he thrust the car into gear and darted from underneath the restaurant awning. In less than a second, he had completely forgotten about his hunger.

"And when I pulled forward guess what I saw?" Diller asked Shelly after wolfing down his spaghetti dinner. Rattled since the encounter with the paw, he'd spent the rest of the day locked in his office, staring at the hotel's TV monitors. He wondered if what he'd experienced was something he should share with his coworkers or a secret better kept to himself. He hadn't even been sure he was going to mention the incident to Shelly until he remembered that eating dinner together was too often shrouded in uncomfortable silence.

"I don't know, Dad," she replied, heaving a sigh.

Diller found that the older Shelly became the more difficult it was to connect. At fifteen she had entered a mercurial phase of development where she was more and more mysterious by the day. He loved her enormously and provided her with all the security she could ask for, but he sometimes worried that Shelly needed more than love and security, though he wasn't sure what that more was. He now noticed that he grew anxious around her, mostly because his attempts to find out who she was only caused aggravation. In response, he found himself actively resisting an interest in the things she did as a way to ward off the inevitability of her rapid withdrawal.

Shelly twirled spaghetti around her fork a few times and then snipped the dangling red nest with a large pair of scissors. The scissors trick had been Maria's idea, conceived at a time when their daughter's inability to draw the connections between fork twirling, noodle mass, and mouth size was still a charming miscalculation. At that time, Maria still smiled and winked at Diller across the table. Later, when Maria started wearing a hat indoors, she sat across from him and smiled a haunting smile while slowly disappearing like the Cheshire Cat. Now Maria didn't smile or wear a hat or sit anywhere at all. Now he couldn't see her, and neither could Shelly.

"You're not even going to guess?"

"No," she said.

"I saw a bear," Diller said, hoping to shock her into taking an interest.

"A bear?" Shelly wasn't buying it. She rested the scissors on the edge of her plate and turned her gaze to a fashion magazine spread open on the table. She flipped pages, releasing a nimbus of perfume. The smell was strong and lusty, clashing with the wholesomeness of garlic bread and tomato sauce.

"Snout, claws, pink tongue, everything," Diller added. "Taking orders, making change. One-hundred percent bear."

Shelly rolled her eyes back to the magazine. "I don't believe you."

Silence followed. Down the hall, a phone rang. Without asking to be excused, Shelly dashed from the table. Diller stabbed another meatball, ate it slowly, and then hollered, "You in there and me out here isn't my idea of family time."

Shelly returned a few minutes later with a look of annoyance that could have rusted a dime. As she slid back into her chair Diller asked her who'd called.

"Just Chris."

"Oh." He wondered if Chris was a *Christopher* or a *Christina*, but he didn't ask. He'd already put one question to her and she'd answered without objection. Another might earn him a surly look. *Or worse*, he thought, eyeing the scissors.

Across the table, Shelly flipped through the magazine, and with each turning page the kitchen smelled more and more like a botanical garden until it didn't smell like a garden at all. It just smelled wild.

He didn't have the heart to tell Shelly how strange her continued use of the scissors was, and if it had been confined to trimming spaghetti he wouldn't have cared. Around the time Maria's health took a turn for the worse, Shelly started carrying the scissors in her back pocket whether there was spaghetti afoot or not. That was six years ago. Clearly, using the scissors had initially made Shelly feel empowered or somehow helped her cope with the loss, but why, at fifteen, was she still using them?

After dinner Diller fell into his recliner for some TV. Nearby, Shelly spread the makings of a project on a folding table. Diller noticed the scissors, cleaned of marinara, sitting on the edge of the table.

Every year since kindergarten her teachers had asked her to make a collage, so Diller assumed that she was constructing one now. If he'd asked he would have discovered that instead of snipping pictures from a magazine, Shelly was cutting fabric and teaching herself to sew.

When nine thirty rolled around he told her it was time for bed. Shelly whined that she needed to finish her project.

"You need it tomorrow?"

In response, she scooped up her work and left the room, returning a few minutes later with a toothbrush jammed in her cheek.

"It's not fair that I have to go to bed while you stay up as late as you want watching TV."

"I'm watching the news," he protested, which was only partly true. The movie he'd been watching had ended a few minutes earlier. "Trust me. I'd love to go to bed early, but as a parent I'm obligated to stay informed."

"About what?"

"About the world. Let's say, for example, that you wanted to go on a school trip to Transylvania. I'd need to know whether there's some sort of class revolt on the horizon, so I watch the news."

"Transylvania's not even real," she said. "I read *Dracula* last year, and it's fiction."

"Transylvania is so real." He'd only chosen somewhere as odd sounding as Transylvania to lighten the mood, but the ploy was backfiring.

"You must think I'm stupid!" Shelly said, her face flushed. "You've been trying to trick me all night. First that business with the bear, and now this."

"Look at a map!" he said. "Transylvania's as real as Moscow or Arlington or anywhere else."

"We don't have a map," she snapped. "We don't even have a dictionary."

After she'd gone, Diller checked the bookshelves for an atlas or a dictionary. She was right. They had neither. He wondered what it meant that Shelly was growing up in a house without maps or dictionaries. He couldn't say, but he thought he'd better buy one of each straightaway.

He watched the news for a few minutes before growing bored, so he flipped over to an action movie, making sure to keep the volume low.

When Diller first started working in the quality control department at Hotel Cazador he was responsible for monitoring the clocking in and out of more than five-dozen workers. Particularly irksome to Diller's inventorying was that while he had data on everyone else, Wine Guy was technically not a hotel employee, so he didn't punch a time card and was therefore off the grid. Adding insult to injury, Wine Guy didn't follow the dress code, didn't abide by the scheduled tasting hours, and frequently left his post to have flings with inebriated guests.

When Diller was promoted to the management position of Quality Control Auditor he decided to let Wine Guy know that his lack of professionalism hadn't gone unnoticed. Confronting him in the break room, Diller asked where he always disappeared to.

"Oh, you know," Wine Guy said, clicking his tongue. "Here and there. Sometimes more here than there, sometimes more there than here."

"Meaning?"

"Meaning 'around,' I guess." Wine Guy's attitude was so blasé it was almost infectiously concussive. "If you don't like that, just imagine I'm having a smoke."

"For thirty-five minutes?"

"I haven't heard any complaints."

"I'm complaining," Diller said, tapping his chest. "Me."

Wine Guy seemed not to hear him.

The glories of quality control were few and far between, so Diller was thrilled when a few years earlier he'd been invited to speak at Shelly's fourth-grade Career Day.

Gap-toothed and twirling, Shelly stood in front of class and said, "This is my dad. He's a Controlling Oddity." Diller and the teacher laughed nervously, after which he explained that he was actually a "Quality Control Auditor." This made little sense to the children. He explained that every time employees entered a new building they were required to swipe their ID cards, which created a digital record that allowed him to see exactly where everyone was and what they were doing.

"Numbers," he said, "when looked at the right way can tell you a lot about the caliber of your employees."

Other information, like who left chronically late, who arrived suspiciously early, and who didn't show up at all, had its usefulness too. All the data Diller monitored helped decide whether employees should be let go, recruited for managerial positions, or remaindered to perpetual sameness.

At the end of his presentation, one of the children in Shelly's class raised her arm and said, with a disarming confidence, that being an auditor sounded an awful lot like being a spy.

When she came home from school the next day Diller told Shelly they'd be eating dinner at Frontier! Burger. Normally she was home before he was, but today she didn't walk in until close to six. Diller decided not to ask why. Smoothing things over with Shelly by showing her the bear was real and that he hadn't been trying to trick her took priority.

The drive-thru speakerbox greeted them jovially. "Welcome to Frontier! Burger, what can I get you?"

"Was that the bear?" Shelly asked, voice dripping with sarcasm. "The wild animal?" She leaned across Diller's lap and craned toward the speaker. "Oh, Mister Baaaaayyyyeeeer," she sing-songed.

"Stop it," Diller said. "That wasn't him. When the bear spoke it didn't make any sense, just jumbles of nothing."

"Duh. That's because it was a bear," she said.

After ordering, Diller was dismayed to find an ordinary teenage boy with a pockmarked face and bicycle-wreck braces working the drive-thru window. Diller handed his cash to a pink, hairless hand and started to worry that he'd been the victim of a hoax perpetrated by a supremely bored employee in a leftover Halloween costume. The entire affair was too bizarre to believe, wasn't it? How could a bear hold down a steady job alongside people without wanting to eat them? Maybe Shelly was right to think he'd been pranking her.

He was poised to put the car into gear and admit defeat when Shelly leaned across his lap and called to the cashier. "Excuse me, sir? Have you seen anyone matching this description?" From her purse she pulled a shorn magazine page. On it sat a figure, ursine and hunched, lips curled in anticipation of virginal honeycombs. "My dad is under the impression that you guys are running a restaurant *and* an animal sanctuary. He swears he saw a bear here yesterday. Do me a favor, tell him he's crazy, would ya?"

"Ha!" Diller said after they'd parked the car and gone inside, bringing their food with them. Shelly was speechless. Lumbering on all fours in front of the frozen custard machine was a large, wooly black bear. Matted fur, pink nose, claws as long as a lobster's.

"I told you," Diller said to Shelly and her slacked jaw.

When a custodian passed by Diller asked how long the bear had worked there.

"Since January," the custodian said. "And the kiss-ass has already been employee of the month three times." He pointed to a row of plaques above the soda fountain. Mounted on polished oak were a dozen photos of smiling, gawking teenagers and three of the bear. Unlike most of the other employees, the bear was very photogenic.

"Don't the customers think it's a little out of the ordinary?"

"They couldn't give a rat's ass for a pound of cheese," the custodian said. Hustling off, he steered his mop bucket like a gondola.

Shelly wanted to take their food home so she could work on her project, but Diller slid into a booth to study the bear in action. He assumed the bear was being trained how to work a register, though he quickly realized his mistake. The bear was the trainer, not the trainee. When the animal lumbered to the rear grill area, Diller approached one of the cashiers. "Excuse me. I was wondering if you could tell me more about the bear."

The cashier gushed with details. Paulo, as the bear was called, was normally the nightshift manager, which was why Diller hadn't encountered him before.

"He's, like, super remarkable," the cashier said. "Even with his speech impediment I can totally understand him."

Diller wondered why a bear would need—or want—a job. Nobody pays rent in the woods, and with those claws Paulo could hunt down anything he craved. Why swap the freedom of the wilderness for the trappings of the concrete jungle?

When he returned to the booth Shelly wasn't there. Bathroom? Diller thought. Normally, he grew nervous when he didn't know where his daughter was—it had been that way ever since Maria's illness. But he was so wrapped up in the bear that he didn't notice Shelly had been gone over twelve minutes, which—he knew from his work at the hotel—was exactly the amount of time needed to smoke a cigarette and wash off the smell.

"Anything exciting happen with our little friend?" Shelly asked when she returned fresh and minty.

"Not really," Diller said, watching Paulo shower a basket of fries with salt. He took another bite of his burrito and studied the bear while Shelly ate her salad. It wasn't until after she'd trimmed the lettuce that he realized she'd used the scissors—not the plastic knife—to cut the wedge into manageable pieces. He reminded himself to have a talk with her about the scissors when they got home.

"Which is stranger?" Diller asked. "That the bear can talk or that he's working fast food?"

Shelly chewed her salad slowly. "Why would it be weird for him to talk?"

He stared at her as constellations of freckles jounced in rhythm to her chewing. "Because bears can't talk."

She looked at him quizzically and swallowed hard. "Of course they can."

Diller pulled the dictionary from the bookstore bag and found the B tab. He read the definition aloud for both of them to hear: "Bear: any of a family–*Ursidae* of the order *Carnivora*—of large heavy mammals of America and Eurasia possessing shaggy hair, rudimentary tails, plantigrade feet, primitive language skills . . ." Primitive language skills? What in the world?

Shocked, he nearly dropped the book. "I know something you don't know," Shelly bragged, laying out her project on the table.

Diller felt ill. As if he didn't worry enough about being a single parent, now he was confronted with the very real possibility that he knew less about the world than the person he was trying to raise. How much more didn't he know? Mountains, probably. And some of these things might be important to pass onto a child so she didn't trust the wrong boy and end up in the trunk of a car or sold into human bondage. He started to worry that the things he was ignorant of without even knowing he was ignorant of them could fill an ocean. And it was in this ocean, on a raft made of shoddy materials, that he feared Shelly might drift away.

At nine thirty Shelly went to bed on her own, leaving Diller in the company of his shock and his recliner. Hoping to find distraction in the TV, he soon drifted off to sleep only to be jerked awake some time later by the sound of a door or a gate closing, followed by scampering footsteps. The last thing he remembered before waking was the feeling of being inside a room full TVs, each one framed by a shaggy mane.

Diller shot out of the recliner, then waited patiently for more sounds so he could lunge toward them. Had he heard robbers entering his home? A scampering animal? Or a child sneaking out for a night of mischief?

He found none of the above. The front door was locked and Shelly was fast asleep in her room.

At work the following day he decided to poll a few of his confidants about the bear thing, even if it meant being made fun of for his ignorance. It seemed that everyone, even Guillermo, who had grown up in a remote village in Guatemala, knew that bears could speak. Diller didn't even know there were bears in Guatemala.

"*Claro que si los osos hablan,*" Guillermo said. "The bear in my village, he talk *a lot*. He go blah blah blah and chat you up all the day. Some people think this bear talk the future."

"The future?"

"Yes. The future. He gypsy bear."

During his lunch break Diller logged onto his computer and searched the Internet for "bear" and "talk." The search yielded six million hits. Scientific studies, master's programs in Bear Linguistics, even conspiracy theorists proposing humankind evolved from bears, not apes. Overwhelmed by the amount of information on the subject, he let out a frustrated groan, feeling as though he'd failed to learn an elementary truth about the world, something as simple as where ice comes from or how babies are made.

"Life got you down, amigo?" Wine Guy asked, popping his head into Diller's office.

If anyone had asked Diller to picture a psychiatrist, he would have thought of a small man with a wiry goatee or a high-foreheaded woman with salt and pepper curls. And though Wine Guy, whose real name was Leon, was the last person Diller would have imagined talking to about his personal life, he found himself confessing all of his insecurities about the talking bear to this charming man in a leather jacket and a Deep Purple t-shirt. Leon didn't have any kids of his own, but he advised Diller against setting the bar of his parenting skills too high.

Later, after much coaxing, the two men passed a bottle of wine back and forth in the back of Leon's van. Diller thought the van—decorated with a broken-down sofa, a TV, and shag carpet on the walls—looked more like a college dormitory than a conveyance. There was something cool about its trashiness that was just now growing on him.

"I used to be a lot like you," Leon said, opening another bottle of wine. "Stressed all the time, workaholic, worried I didn't know what was going on in the world. I muddled over all the impossible questions. Why do bad things happen to good people? What does outer space smell like? Who built the Grand Canyon? Then one day I asked myself, what can I actually *understand*? What can I really *know*?"

"And?" Diller asked, slugging wine from the bottle.

"Myself. The only thing I could absolutely wrap my mind around was myself. *My* motives. *My* actions. *My* reasons. In that moment I discovered the principle I live my life by today: in order to make sense of the world and the events that happen in it, you have to be the cause of those events. You can't just sit back and enjoy the ride or hang on in fear. You have to be the ride. And that's exactly what you need to do, my man."

Noticing Diller's skepticism, Leon handed him a piece of paper with his telephone number on it, delivering it with a sly wink. "When you think you're ready, call me and I'll show you what I mean."

After getting off the phone with Leon, Diller called Shelly into the kitchen. She was in her bedroom and said she'd be out in a minute. It had been a week since Diller's van party with Leon, and in that time his feelings of insecurity about the bear hadn't diminished. So he called Leon, who asked for Diller's address and said he'd be there in ten minutes.

Diller had a $20 bill ready to give to Shelly so that she could order a pizza for dinner, but when he saw her wearing an off-the-shoulder satin gown, black and flowing, he completely forgot what it was he'd intended to say. The dress was formal but eccentric. The ruffled sleeves were cut short, and the back was partially exposed, tapering to a V just below her shoulder blades.

"What in the world?" he said. "Where'd you find that?"

Shelly spun around for him, modeling the dress. She'd put on makeup too, just a little shadow around the eyes and some lipstick. "I didn't find it," she said. "I made it from an old pattern I found in mom's stuff. What do you think I've been working on this whole time?"

"I . . . I didn't know."

"You didn't ask," she said.

Diller silently admitted that she was right.

"Listen," she said. "I have a favor. Chris is going to be here in an hour, and I was hoping you could take a few pictures of us without weirding anybody out."

"Chris?"

"My date for the dance."

Suddenly Diller remembered the banner he'd seen a short time before. He took a moment to absorb everything—the makeup, the dress, the dance. It was the second time in as many weeks that he felt he had overlooked something obvious—first the bear, and now Shelly's project. For somebody whose job it was to watch others, he'd really been in the dark about what was happening under his own roof. From now on, he told himself, he'd do a better job of paying attention to—

A loud blast of horn drew their attentions to the window. Outside, Leon's van idled in driveway. Heavy metal music rocked the black chariot and wisps of smoke trailed from the cracked windows.

"What in the world is that?" Shelly asked as though she were seeing a ghost.

"A friend from work," Diller said. "We were going to grab a beer."

She pointed at the throttling van. "You're actually going to get inside that thing? It looks like a coffin."

"Well I was. But now that Chris is coming . . . and the pictures . . . I'll just have to tell Leon another time."

"Leon? The Wine Guy? I thought you hated him?"

"Turns out he's not so bad," Diller said. "He doesn't know much about the Grand Canyon, but he's a good listener."

"This is too much," Shelly said, enjoying the situation far more than Diller was comfortable with. "Who would have ever thought my dad would be hanging out with the bad news headbanger and his deathmobile? I can't wait to see what's next."

The horn blared again, long and steady.

"I'm just going to tell him we'll hang out another time."

"No way," Shelly said, pushing her father out the door. "This is so rich I'd never forgive myself I didn't let you go through with it."

"But what about Chris and the pictures?"

"That's what tripods are for," Shelly said, waving goodbye. "Don't stay out too late, dear." Her voice dripped with satirical motherly charm. "Make smart choices."

Leon promised he would tell Diller what adventures were in store after a few motivational drinks at a nearby tavern called The Campfire. A few turned into six or seven. Around nine thirty the two men climbed back into the van. Leon turned the key and music blasted. As he drove, he passed Diller a page of poorly scrawled directions. Diller asked where they led. Leon smiled eerily, arched his eyebrows, and said, "That's where *it* lives. The bear."

"How do you know?"

"I followed him home from work yesterday," Leon said, as though tracking bears was as common a pastime as chess or online poker.

"What for?"

The van careened wildly, clipping a stop sign with its bumper and knocking it to the ground.

"To prove to the bear who knows best, that's what for."

Diller sat in silence for the next few minutes not really knowing what to say. Then, they arrived. Leon threw the van into park and in one fluid motion he grabbed the rifle from the backseat and bolted from the car. Up to this point, Diller had pretended he hadn't seen the gun lying across the seat. The time for pretending was over.

Obscuring himself behind a small hedge, Leon yelled for Diller to join him, which Diller did if only to stop the other man from screaming before he drew attention. Tossing Diller the rifle, he told him to look through the scope.

"Forget it. I'm not shooting anything."

"Sure. Ok. Just look through the scope."

Diller raised the rifle and put his eye to the glass, making sure to keep his finger away from the trigger.

Through drawn blinds Diller could see the interior of the bear's house, which was shockingly drab. In a living room full of brown corduroy furniture, the TV was tuned to a sitcom. To the side, in a linoleum-tiled kitchen, the bear stood, an apron 'round his neck, cracking a dozen eggs into a bowl.

Diller shifted positions to steady the scope. There was the crunching noise of twigs snapping under joyless weight. His heavy breathing tempered, and he could feel the heat of alcohol on his tongue.

Diller watched as the bear poured the egg mixture into a pan.

"Go ahead and squeeze the trigger," Leon urged. Diller hesitated, long enough to warrant encouraging. "That bear," he snarled in Diller's ear, "made you feel stupid in front of your little girl. Stupid and weak. And what? You're just going to let him get away with that? What kind of a man just lets that go?"

"Don't you need a permit for this kind of thing?" Diller asked.

"All you need to remember is that this jerk made you feel like a bad dad," Leon snapped.

The bear stepped out of the kitchen and sat on the sofa to watch TV while the omelet fried.

"He made you feel like a zero."

Remote in hand, the bear turned up the volume on the TV.

As he passed the scope over the bear's figure, Diller's breathing moved the cross hairs up and down ever so slightly. He wondered if a bear's heart beat on the left-hand side like a man's, or if it was located dead center.

The bear laughed and laughed. It wiped a tear from its eye.

"Do it."

It took only the briefest moment to realize that Leon's plan to murder the bear was ludicrous. Diller didn't want Paulo dead. There was no reckoning to be had, no scale that needed balancing or axe that needed ground. All Diller really wanted was to be a good father to a daughter he'd started to ignore. To know where she was and that she was safe. Paulo didn't enter into that equation at all.

After throwing the rifle in the bushes he fled the bear's property. He tore through thatches of shrub, dashing home at a pace faster than he thought possible. Leon's words echoed in his mind—*"Diller! Don't be a coward!"*—but he kept on planting one foot in front of the other until his key slid into the lock. He was out of breath, and with the haunting taste of the beer he'd vomited while running still in his nose and mouth, but at least he was home.

He scoured the house, knowing well enough that Shelly wouldn't be there, that she was still at the dance with Chris—whoever Chris was—and that because she expected him to be out late she wouldn't be back anytime soon either. Heaving into his recliner, he turned on the news he was so often pretending to watch. He listened as the reporter detailed a local meningitis outbreak. To ease the metallic sting in his lungs, Diller closed his eyes and held his breath.

A small red door appeared before him. Hesitantly, he opened the door and found a high-ceilinged room with whitewashed walls on the other side. Overhead, a lit bulb dangled from a swinging black cord, and in the center of the room was a white bearskin rug. Intuitively, he grabbed the animal's jaw and lifted the rug, discovering a staircase that led him down a dark, musky passage. At the bottom of the stairs he found himself surrounded by a dozen taxidermied grizzly bears, each one posed in a different expression of monstrosity, arms raised high, teeth exposed. Nestled in the belly of each bear was a small black and white monitor, and as he approached the monitors he saw that each one displayed a different image of Shelly in an act of impropriety—Shelly shooting drugs in the girl's room, Shelly robbing a 7-11, Shelly on her knees in a dark alley, crouching behind a row of oozing garbage cans.

Resolvedly, Diller turned away from the monitors and climbed out of the room, leaving the broadcasts of worry behind. When Shelly came home a few hours later, he was there waiting for her and he was calm. He smiled as she locked the door behind her, and he asked her to tell him all about the dance and her evening with Chris.

Custody

Maya Perez
Michener Center for Writers; MFA

Sabine was to meet Rocco at the Starbucks on the second level of Heathrow Airport. From there, they would fly to Namibia together. She had asked if she couldn't just meet him after he went through security—he was fourteen years old, for Chrissake—but Mark had insisted she meet them in person. "You're taking our son to Africa, Sabine. I'm not going to just send him off into the airport by himself."

And so, after arriving from JFK, Sabine had left the concourse—groaning as she saw the long line waiting to go through security—and gone to meet them at the coffee shop. Rocco was playing a video game, Mark reading a newspaper, and Claudia, his new wife, was on her iPhone. Of course she was there. When Claudia posted photos of Rocco, she always tagged Sabine, as if to show everyone how secure and generous she was with her family. Sabine would study the photos, imagining the life in motion surrounding them that had been stilled momentarily. She would hover her cursor over the button, but could never bring herself to untag her name.

Mark had been promoted and transferred to the MasterCard office in London ten years ago. They already had been divorced a year then and she stubbornly had refused any alimony, which, at the time, had left her living in a studio apartment in Queens. Her housing situation, coupled with her twice-weekly therapy appointments, was what decided that Rocco would live with Mark, just temporarily, until she sorted her situation out. And then Mark had met and married Claudia, a former hand and hair model turned Vice President of Technologies, and it soon became permanent. Claudia was lean and glossy, all parts colored within the lines. Sabine would like to think it was because she never had children, but she knew that when Claudia did—and she would—her body would quickly return to its slender shape. Just as Sabine had always had the body she had now. She had lost weight after having Rocco. Breastfeeding had sucked the calories out of her and his colic had required miles of stroller pushing through the days and nights. It was the only thing that had soothed him. But she had gained back every pound within a year.

Seeing Rocco—my God, he was so tall! She could actually see *man* in him!—she threw her arms wide. He reluctantly stood up and let her hug him.

"You're taller than me! When did this happen? Oh, no. You hug me back."

He gave her a concessionary pat on the back, then sat back down and resumed his video game. Mark nodded at her in greeting. "Sabine."

"Yup!" she replied with a big, tight smile. "It's still my name!"

Sabine would sometimes try to remember being married to him. She knew they had had inside jokes and intimacies. She could even conjure an image of the two of them laughing but, for the life of her, she could not remember a single one. What had they talked about? Three years of marriage, and two years together before that, but she could call up no memories of them.

Only Claudia smiled at her. "What an exciting adventure you two are going to have. Why don't you sit and have a coffee with us? Darling, get her a chair." She rested her long fingers on Mark's arm.

Sabine stayed standing and waved her boarding pass at them. "We should get going. There's a long line at security and it took me forever to get out here."

Mark made no acknowledgment of this inconvenience.

Sabine looked at her son. "Rocco, you have everything? Why don't you say goodbye to your dad and Claudia now. We need to go."

Pocketing his game, he stood. "It's Rocky now."

"Rocky?"

"Oh, his friends came up with it. I like it. It sounds tough." Claudia also stood and took Rocco's face in her hands. "We love you, Rocky. You're going to have such a great time with your mom and we can't wait to hear all about it when you get back."

"You're not bringing that phone, are you?" Sabine asked. "Rocco, we're going on a safari! You don't want to have your head buried in, in electronics. Leave it with your dad."

She balked at his scowl. But, really, this was their trip! She had started an account for it four years ago, when they had spent the summer poring over wildlife books at the library in the late afternoons and pushpin-ing the map of Africa that covered half the wall of his bedroom in her apartment. That had been the last summer he had spent with her before summer camps and trips with friends' families became the preferred vacations.

After he had returned to London, she'd researched the various countries to decide where they would have the best chance of seeing all the animals on their list. Though she was tempted to take him to Kenya, where she had spent her junior year abroad in college, she decided instead that they should discover a new country together. That and the Kenya safaris were too expensive. So, they were going to Etosha National Park in Namibia.

Mark folded his paper and stood up to grip Rocco's shoulder in a hug. "He's fourteen, Sabine. Let him take the game."

After writing their passport and address information in the registration book at Halali Camp, Sabine glanced up and smiled at the stone-faced receptionist.

"We're hoping to see lions. It's my son's first time to Africa."

Sabine could sense Rocco bristling at her offering him up like this, but he said nothing, just continued to study the scat identification poster on the wall. The receptionist's face remained impassive and she handed Sabine a photocopied hand-drawn map of the campsite and, with her red pen, circled site #19.

"The gates open at 6:30 and close at 17:35. You must stay inside your car and on the roads in the park at all times or you will be fined and expelled from the park. You must be inside the gate before 17:35. If you are here after, the gate will be closed and you must flash your lights and toot your horn."

Rocco moved closer to the counter, intrigued by the threat of ominous repercussions. The receptionist looked up at Sabine from the map to emphasize her warning with eye contact. "If you are late, you will be fined and we have the right to expel you from the park."

Sabine disregarded the threat and pointed at a flier underneath the glass on the counter. "Can I book a massage?"

"The girl is not here."

"Well, do you know when she'll be back?"

"She won't be back before you leave."

"Got it. Well, thank you for being so helpful and so . . . *friendly*."

Sabine turned away from Rocco and the woman to shove the map and their passports into her bag. She had known as soon as they drove into the park, where smooth paved asphalt immediately gave over to a road of white rocks and dirt, that she should have gone with the four-wheel drive truck instead of the compact blue car. She had never even heard of an Opel Corsa, but she had been so sure that the man at the rental car company was just trying to upsell her.

The receptionist hesitated for a moment, and then said, "She is gone to visit her family in South Africa."

Sabine stood there dumbly nodding, trying to calm herself.

"There are many lions here. Many lions. You will see them."

"Thank you," Sabine whispered and walked out. Rocco followed her, though with enough distance between them that, to a stranger observing, he could pass for traveling alone. It was a distance he had established at Heathrow Airport.

The rugged, young salesman at REI had told her she would not have any trouble putting the tent together. "Seriously, a monkey could do it," he had said as he rose up and down on his toes, flexing his calves. Not wanting to chance learning in front of other customers that her construction skills were less than those of a monkey's, she had gone ahead and purchased it. Now putting it together for the first time, she was relieved to find that he had been correct.

"We're *both* sleeping in there?"

If Rocco were traveling with his father and Claudia, they would be staying in one of the resort lodges. They would have their lunch and dinner served in a quiet dining room with waiters in stiff white uniforms. Breakfast would be boxed in tidy, white cardboard, stacked on a safari bus that pulled out at dawn. It would be served with silver pots of coffee and tea under the flat, branched canopy of an acacia tree. They would sit on a blanket watching the sunrise over the savannah, while all of the animals gloriously gathered at the watering hole for the perfect photograph, the same photo that would be their Christmas card.

"Yup. And it's a good thing, because it's supposed to get pretty cold at night."

Across their lunch of salami and cheese sandwiches, Sabine watched Rocco's thumbs pound and jerk as he played his videogame.

"How are you feeling about school?"

He shrugged.

"It's your last year before high school."

"Secondary school."

"Right. Are you excited? Nervous?"

He shrugged again.

"Are there any girls you're interested in?"

He didn't respond.

"Rocco? I just want to know what's going on in your life."

He sighed and looked up at her.

"It's Rocky. I go to school. It's fine. I have mates, both boys and girls. What else do you want to know?"

He returned his attention to his game.

"I want to know who your friends are and what you do together. How's your friend, Andrew, or Anders? Do you still hang out with him? Is he still into Star Wars?"

"I haven't been friends with Anders since I was twelve."

"Okay, well, I'm glad we're all caught up."

She pushed her fingers against the rough concrete of the table then looked up at the sound of a vehicle approaching. It was a safari bus pulling in.

A thick layer of white dust covered the vehicle. It grazed the tree branches and barely missed the roof overhang of the washroom before shuddering to a stop. The passengers emptied out quickly, as if they had been squeezed together, waiting at the door. They stretched and looked around at the campsite, shielding their eyes from the bright heat with their hands. After the last of the group eased off the bus, three male crew members in dark green t-shirts jumped out and began unloading the undercarriage. Tents, sleeping mats, sleeping bags, tables, and cots were dumped onto the white ground.

Watching from her collapsible chair at site #19, Sabine was awed by their efficiency and the extent and enormity of their outfit. Even Rocco was compelled to look up from his game as the crew set up camp.

One of the crewmen slid out a large crate from the undercarriage and removed two handfuls of cucumbers, a bag of avocados, several heads of lettuce, and some other items she was unable to see. His face was mostly in profile and hidden by the shade. He placed the vegetables into a cardboard box and carried it to the little screened-in washroom connected to the restrooms. The screen door thwacked shut behind him as he disappeared into the dark.

The passengers from the bus wandered about the camp. Their directionless drifting reminded Sabine of babies trying out their legs. While the crewman in the kitchen remained hidden in the dark interior, the other two men had set the dining tables, gotten all of the cots up and erected more than half of the tents.

The cook, as Sabine now thought of him, opened the screen door and called to the two men who ran to help him. Back and forth, they carried platters from the washroom-kitchen to the long table. An older man with a fanny pack and a visor walked over and spoke with one of the men, then turned and called out to his group. In Spanish? Italian? She couldn't tell. As the tourists made their way to the banquet, Sabine stood up.

"I'm gonna go wash the plates and then we'll go. We should still be able to get a good three hours in the park."

Sabine clinked the metal plates together noisily as she opened the screen door.

"Oh, I didn't realize someone was in here. I'll just go use the . . ."

The man, a boy, really, she saw now that she was closer, glanced up with a smile. He had a wide mouth and eyes that were just a tinge lighter than one would expect. He wasn't Charlie.

She had known it wasn't him, known it *couldn't* be him, even from the distance. But still, there was a similarity. They had dated the last few months of her junior year in Nairobi, and it had been all the more intense because of the timer on their relationship. The question suddenly occurred to her: had she come back in the hopes of seeing him? No, she had come here for Rocco. It wasn't even the same country, in fact there were well over two thousand miles between them. She had come for Rocco.

"Come in, come in. There's plenty of room."

Sabine took her watch off and set it to the side of the sink. She turned the tap and water shot out of the spigot, spraying all over her shirt. Turning it down, she glanced over to see if he had noticed, but his head was turned, focused on cleaning up his area and organizing boxes for future meals. He was lean and short, though still taller than her. His skin was dark and his hair short. He couldn't be more than twenty-five.

"When did you get here?" Sabine asked.

"We come today. Just now. And you?"

"Yesterday. Did you come from Windhoek?"

"No, we started in Gaborone, but this group, they are from Spain. They are Spanish. Where are you from?"

"The United States."

"Obamaland! Which state?"

"New York."

"Big Apple. Empire State Building. Jay-Z. Very nice."

She laughed. "Are you from Namibia?"

"No, just for the tours. I come from Zambia."

She had taken as much time as she could with the dishwashing. There were just the two plates and they had held only sandwiches at that.

"Well, we're going to go into the park now. Bye."

He turned back to his station and she watched the cords of his neck flex, long lines that disappeared into his shirt.

"What's your name?" she asked.

The way he looked back, she could tell he thought she already had left. She was relieved when his face opened into that beautiful smile again.

"Penny. What is yours?"

"Sabine."

She shifted the plates into her left hand and gave a little wave with her right. "It's nice to meet you, Penny."

Rocco had moved to her seat and was hunched over his phone. She reached out and covered the small console with her hand. He looked at her with a raised eyebrow, a skill she guessed he had put many hours into mastering. She sighed. "You look ridiculous when you do that. You ready to go into the park?"

Rocco shrugged.

"Is that a 'yes'? Is that what I am to infer from your shrug, refusal to make eye contact, and obsession with your goddamn videogames?"

Rocco rolled his eyes and looked up at the sky.

"Oh, do you pray now? You've found God?" She couldn't stop herself. He stood up and put the phone in his pocket. "Okay, okay. Let's go."

They went into the park, the small car rattling and bouncing across the flat plains, and Rocco marked on the map the roads they took— Rhino Drive, Eland Drive, Dik Dik Drive. They saw countless oryx, zebras, wildebeests, springboks, and one spectacular bull elephant standing by himself, white-gray against the endless, blue sky. Rocco made notations next to each animal on the list in the notebook that Sabine had given him.

"Do you remember when we made that?" she asked.

"Mom, I was *ten*."

At each dead end, they squinted across the steppe and high grass or through the dense clusters of scraggly trees and shrubs. One of the dirt roads went out onto the pan, the hard, dried, white mud that stretched out further than they could see, waves of heat and distance shimmering on the horizon. The road ended in a giant circle, in which to turn around, and it was here that Sabine turned the car off. Safe from the dust, they unrolled their windows and sat in the stillness.

"I'm sorry for blowing up earlier."

Rocco stared out the window, out onto the pan, but gave a small nod.

"It's just that this trip is so important to me. Spending this time with you is so important to me, and I want us to really *be here* together, you know? You've grown so much since Christmas and it feels like every time I see you, you've grown into a different person. I'm scared that one of these visits I won't know who you are anymore."

He didn't say anything.

"Anyway, I've also been thinking that—well, I wanted to talk with you about this before I brought it up with Mark, with your dad, but I wanted to see how you felt about maybe coming to live with me in New York and going to school there. It was always my intention that you would come back and live with me, but Mark and his new wife—"

"She's not his new wife. They've been married for eight years. They've been married for longer than you guys were married."

Sabine looked down at her hands. When did they get so many lines? They looked like her grandmother's hands.

"You're right. I guess I forget that."

She lifted her head and studied his profile. He had her dark, deep set eyes and full brows, but the rest of his face was all Mark, his long and narrow nose, sharp cheekbones, and his almost nonexistent lips.

"But what do you think about that? There's a good school in biking distance. You have your room . . ."

"I want to stay in London with Dad and Claudia."

"Well, you don't have to decide right now. I just wanted to bring it up. You've got plenty of time to think about it. It wouldn't even be until next summer, anyway."

"I don't want to leave my school and my friends."

"You'll have to go to a new school for high school, anyway, you know. And you'll make new friends."

He turned to her. "I don't want to move."

Sabine smiled to herself stupidly as he turned to look back out the window. She felt tears pricking at her eyes again and stepped out of the car.

"We're not supposed to get out of the car."

She closed the door behind her and, stepping to the front of the car, reached her arms up to the sky and out wide. She closed her eyes tight, then opened them and looked out. There was nothing. No bushes or shrubs. No grass, not even tiny clumps. No hills or rocks, just flat, cracked, white earth in every direction. She stepped over the small rope delineating where cars were not to cross. Just standing on the other side, she felt lighter. Inspired by the vastness of the pan, she took a couple of steps.

"You're not supposed to go out on the pan."

She started running.

"Mom!"

She was running hard. With each stride she reached her legs out as far as they would go.

"We're gonna get in trouble!"

She wished she could run faster. She wanted to run across the plain until she vanished into the ripples of heat. Her chest hurt and she knew she looked ungainly and not at all as she did in her mind's eye, where her legs were lean with sinewy muscle. Her waistband cut into the folds of her stomach. She could feel the fat of her bottom bouncing and it hurt.

She gasped and doubled over, resting her hands on her knees. The lines of the pan ran deep and formed geometric shapes. She wondered how much rain it would take to fill them and make the parched ground soft. When she finally had her breath back, she wiped her eyes, stood up, and turned back.

She got back in the car and sat for a moment. Rocco was looking at her, waiting for an explanation. "We're not supposed to get out of the car. You could've gotten us kicked out. They might have cameras out here for all we know."

She laughed, loud and heavy. "Look around you, Sweetie. Where would they put the cameras?"

He glared at her and turned away.

"You should wear a bra. It's kind of gross."

"Oh, Rocco. You are a fun one, that's for sure." She started the engine and turned the car around.

That night they ate their dinner of cold ravioli straight from the can and split a chocolate bar by the light of their headlamps without talking. Nearby someone screamed and laughter soon followed. Against the distant glow of a neighbor's campfire, Sabine made out the silhouette of a baboon racing off with a bag in its hands. Seconds later, another baboon followed. They were terrorizing several of the campsites and she was glad she had thrown their trash in the bin by the washroom.

Sabine and Rocco brushed their teeth and squeezed into the tent. Their sleeping bags swished noisily against each other as they adjusted themselves, trying to find as comfortable a sleeping position as they were able. For a long while, Sabine listened to their breathing in the dark. She tried to match hers to his, but his exhales were too short and she soon gave up.

That night, Sabine dreamed she was getting a massage from three baboons. She was naked, face down on the table and they each worked her muscles with all four hands, deep and kneading. She wallowed under their manipulation and groaned with pleasure. Why had no one before ever thought to train monkeys to give massages, she wondered. They parted her hair and picked at her scalp. One tugged at her hair and then did so again, harder. Another grabbed a fistful and gave a violent pull.

They slapped the backs of her thighs, pulled the cheeks of her bottom apart and poked and probed with their bony fingers. She felt the urge to defecate and was horrified.

She lifted her head and through the spa door window saw Mark and Claudia sitting in the airport café. But the café was outside and they were radiant, drinking Limoncello under the fading afternoon sun. It was the tall, smoky glass bottle of his favorite brand, the one she and Mark had drunk countless glasses of while on their honeymoon in Sardinia. They couldn't hear her, but still she choked back her shouts. She was embarrassed for the mess she had again found herself in. She wanted to think it would be gratifying for them to see her like this, but knew that Mark, too, would be embarrassed and Claudia's reaction would be even worse. She would be sympathetic.

The baboons' grunts became shrieks. They yanked at her toes, pulling them apart and the pain was unbearable. She was screaming now and didn't care who heard, but they kept pulling and she heard a pop. She tried to get up, but they were jumping on her, laughing hysterically, and baring their teeth.

All the while, Rocco sat intently playing his video game on the floor, the same yellow-flowered-print linoleum of her grandmother's kitchen. He never looked up but she knew he heard her, knew he knew what was happening.

Sabine woke up sweaty and constricted in her sleeping bag. Rocco slept deeply beside her, his mouth open, his breath sour, like spoiled milk. She pulled her hand from her sleeping bag and traced his face with her fingers. His skin that used to be so smooth was raspy with acne and the promise of facial hair. He wore deodorant now and she hated that it masked his real smell. Leaning over him, her nose suspended over the crease of his neck, she inhaled his musky scent, mushroomy and earthy. He'd smelled the same as a toddler. She kissed his cheek, holding her lips on the tender skin until he murmured in his sleep and rolled over, away from her.

Sabine and Rocco had had their condensed-milk-sweetened tea and hardboiled eggs early, so they could go through the gates the moment they opened. They had shivered in their fleece jackets, but now, in the afternoon heat, they were both down to their t-shirts and shorts.

They had seen so many zebra and antelope that they no longer stopped or even slowed when they came across them. "Antelope fatigue," she said to Rocco. Sabine already had replaced one memory card in her camera. Occasionally, they came across a convergence of vehicles and knew something unique had been spotted: elephants, giraffes, and twice a rhino, but she wondered if it was the same rhino. Didn't they take that other road, the far one, earlier? She tried to make out the shape of giant felines on the termite mounds and in the shadows of the acacia trees, trying to will them into sight.

Sabine was tired of driving, her back and neck sore from the bouncing and being so alert for rocks and ruts. They passed the safari bus at one point; she had watched it approaching from the distance. The driver recognized her from the camp, returned her wave, and stopped.

"Have you seen any lions?" she asked through their open windows, glancing behind him.

"We saw a male lion with his kill, a wildebeest, but too many buses came and he dragged it into the bush."

He tilted his head back. Someone was talking to him from within the bus, but she couldn't see who. He turned back to Sabine.

"He is just down this road and turn right at the second marker. There's some small trees and after some bushes. That's where we saw him. Good luck."

The bus drove off, blowing up dust.

They had no luck finding the lion, but saw some dark swathes on the grass near a bush and felt certain it was blood from the wildebeest. Otherwise, there were no remnants.

The sun's orange glare suddenly blinded Sabine and she had to flip down the visor. She glanced at the dashboard clock. It read 4:40, but none of the hands were moving. Their speedometer broke when they went over a particularly nasty bump earlier and its needle now swung frantically. The clock must have broken, too.

Sabine remembered that she had left her watch by the sink in the washroom yesterday and glanced over at Rocco's bare wrists.

"What time does your phone say?" Sabine asked.

"It's dead," he said. "We have to be back at the camp by 5:30."

"5:35. I know. We'll go back now. I don't think it stopped too long ago, anyway."

They retraced their route and had been driving for about twenty minutes—the only other vehicle they saw was a bus in the distance, a plume of dust giving it the appearance of another animal on the savannah—when Sabine noticed that the car was pulling left and two new sounds, a flapping and a grinding, had joined the sound of the tires crunching over dirt road.

Sabine stopped the car and, after a quick glance around, got out. The front left tire was completely flat and the metal rim bent. "You have got to be kidding me," she muttered. She stood up and walked to the back of the car. "We've got a flat tire." Rocco's eyes widened and she made an effort to act nonchalant. "It's no big deal. We just need to change it."

She opened the trunk and pulled out the spare and set it on the ground. She looked for the jack, but the only other things in the trunk were their bags and the cooler.

"Would you get the manual out of the glove compartment?" she called up to Rocco.

Sabine ran her hands along the plastic side paneling looking for a groove that would signify something tucked within, but there was nothing. She walked back around and sat in the car. Rocco was flipping through the manual pages and she held her hand out. "Let me see."

She found the page she was looking for and handed the book back to Rocco. "I'm gonna need you to read the instructions to me while I do this."

She got in the backseat and looked around for a knob or lever to release the seat. She yanked at it hard, but it wouldn't give. The sun cast a wide band across the seat.

"Damnit. Can you help me back here? I can't figure out how to fold the seat down and the jack's behind it."

Rocco climbed between the two front seats to the back, and in the process, knocked her chin with his knee.

"Ow! Why didn't you just get out?"

"What if there are lions?"

Scooting over to make room for him, she glanced outside. The pale grass swayed and glowed under the waning light. The acacia green was rich and vibrant against the slate blue of sky. Wildebeests and zebras grazed in the distance.

"I don't think they'd be so calm if there were lions around."

Rocco studied the backseat and looked for a lever in the same places she did. He then reached under the seats and pulled something. The bench slid forward and the back leaned in. He tried not to smile, but Sabine could tell he was pleased and felt a surge of affection and pride for him. "Good work."

Hunched outside by the tire, she put the jack together and called out, "See if you can find a couple of big rocks to put behind the tires. It'll keep the car from rolling."

Sensing no movement, she looked up. Rocco sat in the passenger seat looking out at the savannah.

"You can't sit in the car while I do this. And I need your help. Can you find some big rocks?"

"I'm scared."

"Oh, for God's sake. We need to get this fixed before it gets dark. You think it's scary now? Just wait 'til we can't see out here."

Sabine stood up and searched the ground for rocks. There was a small pile back off the road a bit and she walked over. They weren't as big as she would have liked, but she didn't see anything that would work better. She heard a rustling and looked up, shielding her eyes to see better. Some of the wildebeests, about thirty or so, had run off, spooked by something. The zebras stayed put, though a few held their heads erect with noses tilted up to the wind.

Sabine heard a loud crack and whipped around. "Stop! Rocco, stop!"

He had placed the jack under the molded plastic of the car and it splintered when he started lifting.

"You have to put it under the metal. Let it down!"

Panicked, he started winding the metal rod again, but in the same direction and the molding collapsed in further.

"Stop! Stop! I'll do it!"

Sabine dropped the rocks and ran over. She pushed him aside and unwound the jack, lowering it. She ran her hand over the fractured plastic. "Shit."

"Sorry."

"You were reading the manual. It said that. And you also have to loosen the lug nuts first."

"I said I'm sorry."

Sabine sighed. "It's okay. Let's just get this fixed. Would you go get those rocks and put them behind the tires?"

He did as he was asked and then sat on his heels next to Sabine, watching as she readjusted and raised the jack, removed the nuts, lifted the tire, removed the tire and replaced it with the spare. He then rolled the spare to the back of the car while Sabine finished tightening the nuts. Sabine stood and watched him struggle to lift the tire into the trunk. She arched her back, stretching, and that was when she saw them: a lioness and three younger lions.

They were bigger than cubs, more like teenagers—large, eighteen-year-old teenagers. The mother, lying down with one of them on top of her, paused from wrestling. The other two stood nearby and all were watching Rocco as he labored with the heavy tire. The lions were about seventy-five feet away. Where had they come from? How had she not seen them?

"Rocco."

But no sound came out. Her throat ached and refused to swallow. All the liquid in her body had dried up and she couldn't produce even the moisture to wet her mouth. She heard her heart beating far away, down a dark tunnel, long removed from her body.

"Rocco."

This time she managed a whisper, but it was too quiet and he didn't hear her. Rocco dropped the tire into the trunk and clapped his hands together to remove the dirt. At the sound and movement, the smaller lion that had been lying on his mother's back stood up. He and the other two, all in a diagonal line, took several steps toward the car then stopped. The lioness remained prone, but watchful.

Rocco looked at his mother, saw her gray complexion and followed her eyes. He exhaled through pursed lips. Under her breath, Sabine whispered, "It's okay. Just stay cool. Just stay cool."

The lioness stood now and her muscles rippled beneath her smooth, golden hide as she walked toward them. She was huge, nearly double the size of the younger lions. She stopped, sat back on her haunches and yawned. Despite her seeming nonchalance, her gaze was intent and watchful. Ahead of her, the three juveniles took this cue to move up and were now about fifty feet away.

Sabine reached her hand forward and fumbled for the door handle. She found it and opened it slowly. "Get in," she whispered. "Be slow and don't make any sudden moves, even when you're inside. Get in now."

Rocco sidled over to her, bent to fit in the door, and slid in.

"Good. Now move over as smoothly as you can." He had to lift one leg and then the other over the gearshift and when his shoelace caught on the seatbelt latch, he panicked for a moment and jerked his knee high. The lioness was up again and moving toward them. She was still trailing the younger lions, now thirty feet away.

Sabine swallowed and choked on her spit as she eased her body into the front seat. She so badly wanted to slam the door, but forced herself to slowly click it shut. In her peripheral vision, she saw a tear run down into the creases of Rocco's neck.

Sabine reached her hand out, took his and squeezed it tightly. He clung to hers, crushing it. Her bones rubbed together and it hurt, but she didn't pull away. Neither of them looked at the other.

The lions walked up to the car and sniffed at the tires. The lioness, padding behind them, stopped when she was in front of the car, her back and head visible over the hood. She turned her face to the setting sun, her eyes momentarily closed. Then she crossed the road and walked on. Watching her go, one of the younger lions lowered onto his haunches, his tail dancing. He ran and pounced, landing on her back. She turned and batted at him with one of her giant paws. Knocked off, he rolled onto the ground and then pounced again. They play wrestled as they walked into the high grass, ignoring both the other two lions and Sabine and Rocco in the car.

A juvenile grunted and walked by Sabine's door, so close she could have run her hand along his back if the window were down. He walked after his mother and brother and, moments later, the last lion followed. A breeze came through, ruffling the tall, wheat-colored waves and when they again were still, the lions were gone.

Sabine watched for a moment, suddenly and inexplicably wistful. Rocco would never live with her. She didn't even know if she wanted him to. She was ashamed by how infrequently she thought of him when they were apart. And she became anxious when she imagined him in her space. She feared his noises and smells would take over her tiny apartment. In their guesthouse in Windhoek, the bathroom walls were so thin that she had heard the rhythmic slapping of his masturbating while he was in the shower. Her lips had curled in revulsion and she'd been unable to look him in the eye at breakfast afterward. But a child should live with his mother, shouldn't he? She gave his hand another squeeze then let go, started the car, and they drove back to camp through the dark.

The gate had been closed for hours and she flashed her lights several times before honking the horn. The night guard in his dark blue uniform opened the gate and waved them inside. He instructed them to pull over by the reception office and closed the gate behind them. His radio emitted bursts of static-coated words, but Sabine couldn't make out the gender of the voice, much less the words. A receptionist was locking up the office door and called to the guard. They stood talking then approached the car. It was the stone-faced receptionist from yesterday morning.

"You are very late."

"Yes, I know."

Sabine could feel Rocco watching her as she told them that they had had a flat tire and it had taken some time to fix. She said nothing about the lions.

"Look, the tire is in the trunk and I can show it to you, if you want. The rim is bent and we'll have to get it repaired tomorrow. I'm sorry we're late, but there was nothing we could do. I'll pay whatever fine there is, just please don't kick us out. It was an accident and I don't know when we'll ever come to Africa again. It was an accident."

The receptionist studied Sabine's face and then Rocco's.

"Are you all right?"

Her voice was so gentle it made Sabine's eyes tear up and she looked away.

"Yes, we're just tired."

The receptionist spoke to the night guard then turned back to Sabine. "Take your car to the petrol station tomorrow. Joseph will let them know you are coming. They will fix your tire. Good night."

She walked away before Sabine could thank her.

Back at site #19, they ate dinner in silence, sharing a can of baked beans, sardines, and a packet of saltine crackers. Sabine had bought a beer for herself and a bottle of Fanta for Rocco at the general store connected to the reception office and they sat in the dark listening to the night insects and the noises of other campers. They got into their sleeping bags, not bothering to brush their teeth, and were asleep within minutes. Sabine had no dreams that night. Her sleep was heavy, black, and bottomless.

When Sabine woke up and crawled out of the tent, she was disoriented by how light it was. It was late morning already and Rocco was dressed and sitting by the propane tank, heating water for their tea. He gave her a little wave. She looked around the campsite and saw that the safari bus was gone. The tents, tables, and cots were all gone.

Sabine and Rocco ate their cereal and watched the little, yellow weaver birds flit in and out of their giant nest. Most of the other campers had set out on their game drives and when she finished her breakfast, Sabine rested her head back, lulled by the swaying branches and the quiet. She was surprised when Rocco stood up and took her bowl. He stacked it in his and walked across the yard into the washroom. The screen door closed behind him and, for a moment, Sabine could see his silhouette in the shadows before he disappeared into the dark of the room.

OpFor (Oppositional Force)

Shane R. Collins
Stonecoast University of Southern Maine; MFA

Cadet Warren Buehler gathered kindling—dried moss, rotting sticks, some dead leaves—and arranged them into the shape of a teepee like he'd seen on survival shows. He lit a match, held it under the wood, and cursed when the flame burned his finger. He struck two more matches, neither able to light the damp kindling. Finally, he unscrewed the canteen with Rumplemintz and drizzled some over the wood. The fourth match ignited the alcohol and, in minutes, he had a sustainable fire. Using parachute cord and his poncho, Buehler made a makeshift shelter to shield him from the rain. With the remaining cord, he strung a line a few feet over the fire and hung two pairs of soggy wool socks. He sipped Rumplemintz, coughed, shivered, and sipped again. He warmed his hands over the fire and smiled. It was his eighth ROTC FTX and by far the best. Rank did have its privileges.

In the fall, seven months earlier, Buehler had received a $25,000 Career Starter Loan from the army. He spent five hundred on a bass system for his Subaru. One of the speakers blew in December and now it rattled every time he played JayZ. He bought a kegerator for him and his roommates as well as a CO_2 tank, new hoses, a replacement tap, and of course, some kegs. Pabst. Blue Moon. Harpoon IPA. They'd averaged a keg a week. He bought a 40-inch LED TV and a propane grill that he'd forgotten to bring inside over spring break and was now rusted. He had an assortment of late-night infomercial workout equipment. A framed and signed photo of Tom Brady hung on the wall beside his pillow-top mattress. Then there were the more standard purchases: movie tickets, deliveries from Wings and Pioneer Valley Pizza, nights out with friends where he bought round after round of drinks, top-shelf bourbon and private lap dances from strippers. His favorite was Candace. She danced three nights a week at the Gold Club. She had fake blonde hair and fake blue eyes. There was a large birthmark between her belly button and C-section scar. For an extra forty, she'd give him a hand job in the champagne room as long as he brought his own condom.

Buehler dropped a log onto the fire. It popped and sizzled, sparks carried away by the smoke. Under his poncho was his assault pack—a quarter as large as the usual rucksack. There was a five-gallon drum of water, a hand radio, and a First Aid Kit. Only one cadet stopped at his checkpoint.

"Is this Checkpoint Alpha?" Cadet Sanford asked. She wiped a streak of mud off her face as Buehler topped off her canteens.

"No, it's Bravo."

"Oh." She sat under his poncho for a minute, looking at her map and shaking her head.

When she left, Buehler took out his second canteen. Unflavored vodka. He sifted through the contents of his MRE, found a packet of orange drink mix and shook some of it into the canteen. Later, he toasted some marshmallows. Most of them caught fire because he was too impatient.

For Christmas, he bought a new Keurig coffeemaker for his parents and engraved shot glasses for his two brothers. He bought a set of pearl earrings for his girlfriend, Becky, who broke up with him on New Year's Eve a week and a half later. For a few weeks, he hoped she'd surprise him and return the earrings. Now he was happy she'd kept them.

He bought a set of winter tires for his roommate. He bought cigars imported from Honduras and whiskey imported from Scotland. When friends came to his apartment, he enjoyed having them try both. In March, as his graduation and commissioning drew near, he bought framed photos of himself with his friends and family. He sent a photo to his sister of the two of them paddling along the Connecticut River in red kayaks. He sent photos to his brothers of the three of them after a game of Thanksgiving flag football. Their white t-shirts were ripped and stained with grass and dirt. Buehler's lip was cracked, blood dotted his chin. They had broad smiles. He sent a picture to his father of them on a fishing charter. They each held a striper they had caught. The boat didn't have a scale so the two argued every Easter about whose fish was bigger. He'd sent a photo to Becky of the two of them at last year's Big-E fair. He carried her in his arms, one of her shoes—a sparkling silver flat—dangled from her toe. She laughed, open mouthed and unaware of the photographer. She mailed it back to him, the frame cracked, the photo torn neatly down the middle. It made him sad. He wanted people to remember him.

It was the morning after Buehler's FTX fire. He ran from tree to tree, firing his assault rifle from his hip without any concern for tactics, like he was the star of an 80s action movie. He was an OpFor, the make-believe enemy for the training cadets. He pretended to get shot. Clutching his chest, Buehler collapsed to the ground and did a theatrical roll. His rifle slipped from his fingers. A cadet approached and put his knee on Buehler's chest, pinning him. Someone else took his rifle. The cadet pinning him was a first year named Kerney or Krieger. Buehler always mixed the two up.

"You're history, towelhead," the cadet whispered. "You're fried. Ventilated. Toast with a side of bacon."

Buehler's mouth was open and his tongue hung out. He was dead. Some pine needles had stuck to his face during his John Wayne roll. They tickled his nose.

In September, he found out what he had branched: Massachusetts National Guard military police. It had been his first choice. He was ecstatic, relieved. No one got his first choice.

"I made it," he had said to Sergeant Peralta when he found out. He didn't care for the war. He didn't want to deploy or to have to shoot people. Hurricanes, blizzards, power outages. That's what he wanted—to help his friends and neighbors. He wanted to position sandbags to prevent hardware stores from flooding. He wanted to hand out bottled water and MREs and toilet paper. He wanted to help people who wanted to be helped.

"National Guard, huh? Nasty Girls?" The sergeant bit a fingernail and nodded. "They're pretty much the same as active duty. You'll be in Iraq in a year."

"Iraq? Really?"

"Sure," Peralta said. "Iraq ain't a war. It's an occupation. A police action. MPs deploy more than anyone. A year in the sandbox, a year stateside." Peralta scratched at a pimple on his chin.

Buehler applied for a Career Starter Loan later that week.

On Sunday night, after the FTX, he went to Applebee's with the other fourth-year cadets. They ate potato skins and cheeseburgers. They had five pitchers of beer and a round of Jim Beam. Buehler paid the bill.

"To Buehler," cadet Finch said and lifted her glass. "And to another FTX in the books. Our last one together." She smiled as if they shared a secret. "And to the light at the end of the tunnel."

Buehler didn't see it that way. He felt he'd entered the tunnel and the light behind him was growing dimmer and dimmer.

The first thing Buehler had bought was a calendar from *Sports Illustrated*. Girls in string bikinis. It helped him keep track of how many days were left until he commissioned. He crossed out a square each night. One hundred thirty days.

He bought expensive toothbrushes and when he got a cold, name brand cold medicine. He went rock climbing and in October, went to Vermont with Becky for a weekend of snowboarding and beer brewery touring. One hundred and two days.

He bought things he'd always wanted. A Massachusetts pistol permit and a Glock17. An ice fishing kit. A book on New England's best hiking trails. He bought things he'd never use. A hydroponics kit and an empty twenty-gallon fish aquarium collected dust in his closet. Eighty-seven days. A handmade, black leather cowboy hat he wore once to a party. A silver wristwatch that he had left in his will to his older brother. Two pairs of Ray Ban sunglasses. Snowshoes. Forty days.

After Applebee's, he went to the Gold Club and saw Candace. When he walked in, she ran to him awkwardly in her high heels and threw her arms around him.

"You want to go to the Champagne room, darling?"

"Yeah. Can you grab us some drinks?"

He went to their usual corner of the champagne room and sat down on the greasy leather couch. Candace handed him a gin and tonic, slick with condensation, and sipped her Washington Apple.

"I'm commissioning soon," he said. "Next month."

"They sending you to the war?"

He shrugged. "Maybe." His hands were cold. They shook as he set the drink down on the glass coffee table.

Candace put her palm on the crotch of his jeans and rubbed. "What does my baby want tonight?"

His eyes burned, he looked away. He leaned against her, put his fumbling hand on her knee, lay his head on her lap. Her thigh was cold. He was crying now. He couldn't stop. She ran her fingers through his hair, brushed his cheek. He could smell the acrylic on her nails.

"It's okay," she whispered. "It's okay, baby."

He felt better than he had in a long time.

On his way home, he stopped to get gas but his card was denied. He went inside and gave a twenty to the cashier. When he got home, he went online and checked his bank account. He had three dollars and forty-two cents. It was okay. There was nothing left to buy.

He went to his *Sports Illustrated* calendar, crossed out another day, and flipped the page. It was May first. Buehler had twenty days.

A Language Translatable by No One

Courtney Kersten
University of Idaho; MFA

1.

Obviously, when you're mourning, you need cheese curds. You need seven pounds of cheese curds.

You need rhubarb pie and red velvet cake and blueberry cobbler. You need five lasagnas and three bottles of vodka and two tubs of port wine cheese. You need wild rice soup and gumbo. You need daisies and therapeutic candles and an essential oils kit and two copies of the same *Meditations for Men* book and an Islamic prayer rug and a twenty-seven-pound copy of the Bible. You need a wild amount of chocolate. You need stuffed animals holding hearts and a twelve-pack of Coors and posters showing kittens with inspirational platitudes in thought bubbles. You need waterproof mascara and those tiny packages of tissues. And, most definitely, you need seven pounds of cheese curds.

The refrigerator door opens. It's your younger brother. "Who the fuck gave us seven pounds of cheese curds?" he asks.

"Steve," you reply.

The door closes. "Why the fuck did he give us seven pounds of cheese curds?"

Because of the pasteurized milk for Chrissake! Because of the dialogue between the cheese cultures, the salt, the whey, and just the way it sits in the fridge between the pie, the banana bread, and the salmon dip: the fridge sings a language translatable by no one—not even the fridge itself. It's the language of not knowing what to say, not knowing what to do, but watching a car crash and throwing *Donny Osmond: Greatest Hits* toward the scene believing it will help.

I open the freezer door. "We have four loaves of banana bread?" I ask.

My mother would never eat banana bread. She was not a banana bread woman. She was not an Islamic prayer rug woman or a let's sit down and smear lavender on our temples and meditate woman. She was also not a pie person. Pie was something that never happened. She was a let's get drunk and flash our relatives kind of woman. She was a saltines and Cheese Whiz for dinner kind of girl. She mocked sentiment and shushed tears, her emotional world an enigmatic Bermuda Triangle.

The refrigerator door opens. Not-so-baby brother searching for treasure again. "JELL-O?" he asks. He wheels around and places the quivering rainbow in front of me. "JELL-O. What sweet sweet motherfucker gave us JELL-O?"

I stare back. "Your sweet, motherfucking Aunt Bonnie."

Yet, if there was ever a time for our mother to be sentimental, to indulge in those cream puffs she denied herself for the sake of that paisley bikini, to smear patchouli on her temples and meditate for a miracle, this was it. But she didn't let this shit touch her. Not the cards, not the letters, not the bears holding hearts, or even the motherfucking JELL-O. She'd find me bawling, crawling on the floor in devastation, and she'd yank at my elbow, and ask, "What's wrong? Why are you crying?"

Why am I crying? Why aren't *you* crying?

I felt like apologizing to every person who reached out. I imagined my lines: *She really appreciates your thoughtfulness and the Bundt cake you brought; we all do. It's very kind of you. You have to understand her reticence; she's just processing. It's tough news. We have to give her grace. She's just not as emotive as she used to be.*

Not that she ever was. She harbored an unfathomable essence, an impossible poise that required moments of affection to be measured in quality not quantity. She wouldn't coddle every tear but she could stare back and smirk at the men who made lewd comments to her at bars and wink at despair. I envied her stoicism.

Once, she brought me along to the funeral of one of her colleague's fathers with the promise that she'd take me out to lunch and we'd see a movie afterwards. I knew neither the colleague nor her ninety-eight-year-old father but I sobbed through the entire funeral. My mother handed me a tissue and hissed, "Jesus Christ, pull it together! You didn't even know him."

"I . . . know. I can't help it. They played . . . 'How Great Thou Art.' It's so . . . sad."

I often wondered if all of this was really just a giant piece of performance art: my mother had fooled us into believing she was dying. Those cheese curds? Totally orchestrated. The inspirational kitten posters? A complete joke! Us crying? Pfft. Total suckers. The jaundice? It's just stage makeup! That oncologist? He's an actor! And maybe that's the point. Maybe she's trying to make a statement about our culture's fear of death, yet she is facing it and *that* is her artistic statement. I was her curator, collecting moments of half-implied emotion, documenting the objects she used, and the clothing she wore in an attempt to collage an implication of her inner world. Yet, she was a postcard with nothing written on the opposite side: a seemingly void paradise.

I call my father to alert him that I'm showing up at his house with a snot-encrusted chin and a fruit basket. I pull into the driveway and see him through the window: he's sitting in a recliner wearing his camouflage ghillie suit. He wears it for turkey hunting but the ensemble would also be an appropriate choice if you wanted to be a compost pile for Halloween. He waves at me. When I told him the news, he brought over a twelve-pack of Coors, three bottles of wine, and a box of Kleenex. He asked what he could do to help. I told him it would help me very much if he wore his ghillie suit in public one time, just for me. He asked me if wearing it around his yard would count. I said yes.

I wave back and he moves from the chair to meet me outside. He looks like the sixty-year-old love child of John Denver and Chewbacca. It's January in Wisconsin and it's above freezing so that means it's warm. And when it's warm you sit outside and watch your neighbors power walking around the cul-de-sac, giddy and numb, in shorts. We sit in the driveway, open up the cellophane, and each take an orange. I watch him peel the rind, dribbling juice on his hands, and wipe the mess on his suit. Concentrating, he separates the orange into four hunks.

"Dad."

He looks up, and I know he knows we are on the verge of me howling into the sleeve of his ghillie suit in the driveway, surrounded by melting snowmen and orange peels and cellophane, in front of all the neighbors who've crawled out for the sunshine. He swallows a hunk of orange, reaches inside the suit to hand me his handkerchief, and grabs my orange to peel it for me.

"If you were dying you would . . . tell me things, right? I mean, there would be some . . . final words or whatever . . . passed on?"

"Yeah. I mean, of course, I would do that."

"Then . . . why isn't she?"

He pauses. "I don't know." He tosses the peel in the snow and the labrador grabs it. "I mean, you would think if you're dying you'd wanna give some last words to your kids, you know." The lab brings the peel back to him. "But she's just not that way. She's never been. It's a German thing. It's the way she was raised. She's not, you know, expressive."

"But I want her to be. I really want her to. She doesn't even talk about having a brain tumor. Or about dying. She says . . . nothing. She talks about other things."

"Well. I dunno. She gets to run the show; she's the one that's dying. You're just gonna have to live with it being that way." He takes the peel from the dog and flings it into the woods, yelling, "Don't you eat that!" The neighbor lady wearing a Packers jersey and curlers in her hair jogs past us and waves. We wave back. I thank him for wearing the outfit and he thanks me for the fruit and hugs me lopsided, shoving my face in his armpit. Up close, his swamp-creature suit is fetid; it's like sticking your nose between the cracks of an abandoned barn that's been locked and left to collapse. He asks me if wearing the ghillie suit made me feel better and I tell his armpit, yes, very much so, and he lets go. And my father, the one-time Chewbacca, disappears into the garage with the dog following behind. My teeth start to chatter.

I crawl home and onto the closet floor, close my eyes, and grab a canoe paddle. I drift back to that corner of my mind where, for weeks, I've gathered thirty years worth of kisses on my cheek, of gossip shared in vinyl restaurant booths, of rushed "Iloveyous" over the phone, of winks across the room and countless questions—about ovarian abnormalities, about the things I should've said in response to this friend or that man, about family myths, about whether to wear a girdle—and wrapped them together in a lilac, crochet blanket in a wicker bassinet. I stare down at this little mystery, my tiny inheritance, the everything I long to watch ripen and grow, knowing that soon this gift will be hijacked by forces beyond comprehension. With no intellect or care to discern between me and my lapsed legacy, me and my tragedy, me and what I thought was mine, these forces, these apathetic, drooly creatures, will enter the room and go straight to the bassinet. No bargains, negotiations, or trades. Ravenous and resolute, they will take my bundle of should've-been decades and consume her for their own purposes. And I will watch motionless, gagged and bound by my own sorrow. And I will do nothing but fantasize about the things I could say or do to these creatures and prepare to dress my own wounds. Ripped to the bone, bassinet plundered, I will be eaten alive by everything that will never be asked, answered, told, or experienced. My canoe paddle no help to fend off this inevitable abduction.

I wipe my eyes. I need to talk to Ellen. Ellen is my psychologist friend who should be charging me hourly for the number of times she has to talk me into crawling off my closet floor and on with my life. I tell her about the banana bread and eating oranges in the driveway and plotting to battle off slobbery mouths with a canoe paddle. I say, "OhmyGod, I just *keep thinking* what if she has a stroke *tomorrow* or something and *I never told her* how much I love her and *everything*. But, I *can't tell* her this stuff. I, like, can't even get the words out. I've tried! I've tried! Like, multiple times to practice in my closet. And I just cry. And she hates that. So, what. *What am I su—*"

She coaches me to breathe. "Okay. You can't say it. That's okay. That's totally okay. What about writing a letter? You can write her a letter, draft it out, say everything you want to say; maybe invite her to write one back and give it to her—"

"Yes. That's brilliant. You're brilliant. Thank you," I say and hang up. I try to do exactly what she says but I feel like I am ripping off a Hallmark card. All the things that I think will be so intimate sound like an answering machine message. I play with the idea of making a slide show and think about collecting all the tissues I've used in weeping for her in a giant olive jar as a testament to my devastation and, subsequently, my admiration. But instead, I write of my love, my gratitude, and my sorrow for her, invite her to write back to me, and leave the card next to her toothbrush so that she'll see it in the morning.

The next day, I am surveying the bagel sampler someone gave us and she touches my hand and says, "Thank you for the card, Courtney; that's very nice of you." She stares at me and I am tingling with anticipation of the letter she's going to pull from her robe or the kiss she'll smear on my cheek or the card so sentimental it oozes at the creases. She squeezes my hand. "You can have all of my clothes."

Days later, I am exercising my privilege as a daughter to borrow my mother's stuff. I'm rooting through her jewelry armoire and she comes up behind me and pats my back, "Soon, Court, all of this will be yours." I turn around. "And then, in twenty years, you can sell it or melt it down for cash."

"*Mom*. I'm not gonna, you know, melt your stuff down or pawn it. I'll keep it and I'll wear it to . . . to remember you. I'll wear it to remember you." She meets my eyes.

Smoke collects between our gaze and it is there that we embrace each other; it is our ether where we are rabbits sewn together in a fur coat and wedding dresses at Goodwill and salt-and-pepper pop stars playing at county fairs and dead house cats in the street and my mother's copy of *When I Am An Old Woman I Shall Wear Purple* tossed in the garbage and we are not the things we thought we would be when we grew up.

Hot boxed in by her own demise, she knows the cards she holds: step-by-step, this is how you will go. Dumbfounded by the hand she's drawn, clutching to her fortune, her only invariable, she has let everything else go. The periwinkle robe she has worn for weeks—swaddling her astonishing emaciation, grimy with urine and her children's tears, with melted chocolate and crumpled lottery tickets in the pockets—is her white flag. Holding her there, sand slipping through my fingers, I understand her choke hold. She is strangled by an unfathomable grip on a life too green.

She doesn't need to say anything. A single tear forms in her eye and slides down her face. We are silent.

"Mom. Why do you all your friends think you like banana bread?"

2.

The doorbell rings. It's a package from the Netherlands. I open it. Inside are two bags of ground coffee and an aluminum can duct-taped shut enclosing a thin layer of coffee to smuggle a saran-wrapped loaf. The loaf has a powdered-sugar smiley face on it. There is a card inside. "For your Mom."

Too late.

My brother Conrad is at the kitchen table modeling his new funeral suit and jabs his fork into a piece of rhubarb pie. "Okay. Okay. So, nothing can, you know, fix this, but, you wanna know fuckin' what? This shit, *this* shit, at least, you know, temporarily fixes it." He grins and bits of masticated crust fall from his mouth like kids missing the end of a trampoline. "What?"

"Nothing," I say.

I put the pot brownie in my purse and creep into my mother's bedroom. *Soon all this will be yours.* I peek underneath her sink. There is a pair of black tights, the last dose in a three-day yeast-infection-treatment kit, and a card reading: *To My Daughter On Her 25th Birthday . . .* that she had never given me. I open the card.

There is nothing written inside.

3.

Even after our frozen-soup cornucopia is hidden in a freezer-burn dusting and the funeral flowers are long tossed into the woods, moldy and bloated, a police camera flashes upon opening her closet door. *Shoplifter*! *Peeping Tom*! *Snooper*! Rooting through her stuff feels dirty. Sometimes I would sit outside the doorway and ask for permission, a child tapping on glass, salivating with curiosity.

I start with what I can lasso with my foot from outside the closet: new winter boots still in the tissue paper and box. A swimsuit bought on discount, in the plastic bag, to be worn for the next summer that never came, a boxed-up Easter dress for the picnic that never happened. I arrange the boots, the dress, and the swimsuit so that we can powwow together: a triage support group. *She left all of us! She was supposed to wear me!* The Easter dress wails Irish wake style, her boots whimper, the swimsuit has retired to the far corner of the closet to weep. I try to console the clothing and take cover: her abducted decades have burst through the window and tears shatter like glass around all of us wailing on the linoleum.

Shoving the Easter dress inside the boots to quiet it, I hug the whole sopping mess and curl up facing the wall, hoping that the harder I press on the soles the more likely it becomes that she will poke her head out from the closet, like a children's toy that squeaks when you press the belly, appearing to halt our breakdowns. I flip over and stare across the floor.

Her hairs lie in a gentle slumber, at peace with their chemically induced eviction on the linoleum. Mom. I reach out, gather a clump in my hand, and watch the blonde strands fall through my fingers and waft to the floor. Where did you go? I do it again and again and again and again and again: pick up the hair, watch it fall, pick up the hair, watch it fall. Revving up, boiling with the juice that bulldozers and sledge hammers and kids who throw cats into bubble baths run on, I abandon my fellow lamenters; the boots fall to the floor, hair scattering in their quake. I stand up.

Shaking and filthy and wild, I charge in and run my hands over every orphaned item. I will tempt you. I am a thief. I am taking all of your shit. Show up. Stop me. I strip off my clothing, put on her lacy purple lingerie, as much jewelry as my body's surface area can accommodate, her fur coat with the dozens of pills she never took thrust in the pockets, and lay on the floor of her closet spread out like a starfish. Come get me. I'll wait right here. Ground me. Slap the handcuffs on. I close my eyes.

The cameras are flashing yet we both are the ones who are robbed. There are the lights, the conversations burped through walkie-talkies like a Dadaist poem, badges adjusted, pens beating on note pads, driver's-license numbers inscribed, questions asked, tires on snow-packed roads, have a good night, the culprit is let off: illogical allegation. *"Suspect" ate canoe paddle but left all seven pounds of cheese curds? No further action needed.*

Open.

This wasn't a giant piece of performance art. She wasn't hiding out at the neighbor's house or behind the space heater. She wasn't coming back to send me to my room or report me to the police. I could've remained there forever, died there, a bedazzled, skanky starfish in her closet. I stand up. The coat's silk lining is a wet cough against my skin. I look around. It is me alone in a closet deciding what to do with what is left: she is everywhere and nowhere. And the answers to the questions I never asked, the answers to questions she was too ill to have answered—about being a woman, about how to live without her, about where she had gone—hang in the air, tinkering back and forth in their ambiguity, like the naked hangers.

I collect all of her clothing and jewelry, take what I want, and put the rest into the "PERSONAL BELONGINGS" bags I had taken from the hospital and transfer the entirety of my mother's wardrobe into my closet, creating two layers of plastic bags covering the floor. It is their purgatory and the place where a wild possessiveness grips me. Despite keeping about a third of her clothing, preparing to give away the rest for other women to wear feels like I am giving away her secrets. She had owned her womanhood, while I merely poke at the idea of mine with a stick. Her clothing and jewelry are exotic insects cast in amber, her essence trapped behind velvet ropes at an ancient wartime history museum: Incan tomahawks and Viking axes. I have no idea what to do with any of it—she was the warrior; I was the one blubbering about "How Great Thou Art." I abandon my bed and sleep in the closet amongst the bags for weeks hoping that the longer I keep her clothing hostage the more likely it is that it will cough up the secrets of motherless existence.

Then, one day, my closet door opens. Conrad is standing there, looking at me crumpled amongst the plastic bags, where weeks worth of dried snot, an inadvertent mosaic, has marbled their lacquer surface. My breath rattles against the bags. Lodged in my harem of possessiveness, I see the newspaper heading flash in his mind: *Girl Asphyxiated by Closet Full of Garbage Bags.*

"What'cha doing Court?"

"Cry . . . ying."

"What are all these bags?"

"Mom's . . . clothes." I turn to face him and wipe my face in my shirtsleeve. His eyes roam the carnage. "Do you think I'm weird or something?"

"No. Why?"

"Because I haven't . . . taken this stuff to Goodwill or . . . wherever. And it's been weeks. Because I'm sitting here . . . in Mom's clothes. Crying."

I can see him thinking about what the right thing to say is. "No. You know what, Court? You know Mom's friend? Whatsherface? . . . *Cathy Bowe.* Cathy fuckin' Bowe kept that poodle in her freezer for three years after it died. So, you know what? You can sit here for a bit. That's okay, Court. That's just okay." And so I do. And the next morning, I dress up in the things I said I'd remember her by. I crawl out of the closet, and on with my life.

I pull up to the donations drop-off door, open up the trunk, and start to place the bags into a bruise-colored cart the clerk brings out. He watches me and whistles. "Whooooee! You gotta lotta stuff . . . heh, hey! Did somebody die or something?" He laughs, slapping the rim of the cart, looking at me to share his joke. I bow my head. The stillborn future has dissolved into a mist, re-welcomed into the atmosphere, the questions no longer an anchor but the Rosetta Stone to understanding the language of these synthetic fibers, the whisper of sapphire rings, and the exchanges between silk-lined coats and long underwear: the script to her impassive performance art, the opportunity not to surrender but to create.

I look up at him. "Yeah. Somebody did." I give the rest of the bags to him, pull away, drive twenty feet into the parking lot, and roll into a spot, the car idle.

I want to run back. I want to grab everything that was hers and take it back. I want to tear up her clothing, dump out her perfume and cosmetics, grind up her jewelry, throw it in boiling water, let it simmer, and recreate her from the goop. Replica Mother. Magic Mom. You Four Months Ago. Can I do that? Is that possible? Should I have saved everything? What if, one day, that *is* possible and I just screwed it up by giving everything away? I see myself tackling women in the grocery store, tearing my mother's sweaters off their bodies, battling it out in the bread aisle. I see myself buying everything back. I see myself living forever inside my closet nestled into her clothing: make-your-own womb. I see myself trapped as a twenty-something, never being able to grow up without her, and forever begging her clothing to somehow assemble my mother's essence and give her back.

I turn off the car, wrap myself around the steering wheel, and scream.

It was my right of passage. More than the generous amount of pies and parade of hot dishes, more than the obituary and funeral and seeing the county coroner wander in our front door, giving away my mother's clothing to be reincarnated into other women's outfits was final. Wearing her clothing and jewelry was my own reincarnation. I was not a thief or a voyeur; this was my gift. I was the clothing's guide and it was mine.

The squeeze of her sweater stretches across my back. And I feel the last moment I touched her as a healthy, mentally sound woman when she held me so tight and whispered that she loved me so much, that her love was so big, and when she looked above, grinning from that expansive velveteen pool inside her stoicism, she said, "It's like the sky, it's just there, wherever you go."

And I breathe.

I poke my head up.

I hadn't asked the questions, but she had given me the answers.

I go home. And I sit in her closet with the birthday card she never gave me and I fill it with the words of everything she couldn't say.

Electronic Heads

Meng Jin
Hunter College; MFA

1.

On May 20, 1989, four weeks before Feng was due to be born, his mother Xiao Lin checked into the hospital, complaining of labor pains and feeling incredibly lucky. Beijing was a mess. Students, workers, even teachers had abandoned their jobs to shout and sit in the streets, and in Tiananmen Square of all places. They had been at it for weeks. Chanting could be heard at all hours, whether you were by Tiananmen or ten miles away—*Down with Li Peng!* was the latest. Xiao Lin cringed. She was glad that she could refrain from within the neutral walls of a hospital. Not that she expected anything to happen, but as the assistant to the head of the Department of Transportation in the Ministry of the Interior, she welcomed the opportunity to not have to think anything, one way or the other. She could only imagine the grand disarray at the ministry headquarters—whispered rumors, quick accusing glances, and the boss storming in an hour late every morning, turning over tables and throwing files to the floor, red faced and screaming at all of them as if the traffic holdups and street blockages were their fault. It was a wonderful relief, to be on maternity leave.

The contractions were not so bad, really, not much worse than the worst menstrual cramps. They passed quickly and did not come often. As she was not due to have the baby for another month, she thought they were likely not even contractions. But who knew what could happen, her mother-in-law Wei had said. Better to ask the doctors. Wei had moved to Beijing from Diaowo, the village outside of the capital where Xiao Lin's husband Da Ping was from, to look after the mother of her first grandson. Wei was an unusual country woman: not only was she literate, she was a passionate reader of Lu Xun, and thus she preached daily the positive effects of Western medicine, shaking her bottle of aspirin while other old ladies brewed their concoctions of teas and roots. "Don't feed *me* buns dipped in human blood," she'd say when offered a home remedy. And so when Xiao Lin dropped a bowl in the kitchen the morning of May 20 and shouted out in pain, her mother-in-law, running over, leather shoes pattering on tile, had only one thing to say: "They'll get to the bottom of it at the hospital."

And when at the hospital it was confirmed that Xiao Lin was suffering from false pains and could return home, it was her mother-in-law who had insisted she stay. "Best to be close to the professionals," she'd said. Besides, she reasoned to the attending physician, what with the ruckus out on the streets—some other development, the declaration of martial law, had gotten everyone riled up again—it had taken them three hours just to get to the hospital, a trip that normally took less than one. Certainly this kind of stress was not advisable for a woman who was eight months pregnant.

Xiao Lin lay back into her hospital bed and pulled open the bag that her mother-in-law had packed for her, which included not only some hand towels and a bottle of aspirin, but also two books, Lu Xun's *Call to Arms* and Mao's little red one of aphorisms. As Wei left the room to phone her son about his wife's status, Xiao Lin fished in the bottom of the bag and drew out an envelope she had hidden there. She stuffed it under her pillow before Wei returned.

She was not superstitious. Just last week she had happily eaten cucumbers when Wei served them—cucumbers, she had always been told, were a yin food forbidden for pregnant women. She read the newspapers and had even learned quite a bit of English in university; she considered herself a modern woman—she would not want her mother-in-law to think otherwise. It was only in matters of importance that she loosened the belt of logic. Listening carefully for the sound of Wei's footsteps in the hall, she peeked under the pillow and drew out the envelope, opened the brown flap and pulled out the two pictures inside. They were glossy magazine cutouts of an American film star named Robert Redford. In one, the actor squinted into the sun in a beautiful white suit, his arm resting in easy proprietary lines on the hood of a winking yellow sports car, his weight squarely on one hip. In the other he wore a white turtleneck and everything about him was tousled and soft. Her friend Tingting from work, a real cosmopolitan, had given her the pictures months ago when Xiao Lin found out she was having a boy. It was silly, really, that old saying that if you looked at a face long enough when with child, your child would be born with that face. Xiao Lin certainly did not believe it. But she kept the pictures underneath the pillow just in case, and stared at them dutifully every day. For what harm could they do? Wouldn't Wei be happy with a handsome grandson?

The night of June 3, two weeks before Feng was due, Xiao Lin woke from a nap and found that the sheets were wet. Her mother-in-law alerted the doctor. The cramps she checked into the hospital for had not subsided in the previous weeks, flaring and fading one or two times a day. But this was fiercer, more insistent. For whatever reason, however, it was not more painful. Perhaps because she'd had the mock contractions, perhaps because she too found spiritual comfort in Wei's miracle of modern medicine—she did not feel the wrenching, indescribable pain she'd been warned to expect. She did not scream like the women who had passed in and out of her room; screaming did not seem very useful. She closed her eyes and pushed, as if she was taking a long, uncomfortable shit. Within an hour she was dilated—the baby in position, ready, waiting for his cue—she was wheeled into the delivery room, a long rectangle with two rows of empty white beds, and deposited onto a bed by the wall.

Cooperatively, Feng was coming. Wedging down the birth canal head first, facing his mother's back, presenting not one complication. Halfway into the night, when one day was passing into another, Feng's scrunched face emerged from between Xiao Lin's legs with a hearty shriek. The shriek echoed off the gray smudged walls, struck the sweating windows and slipped out through the crack and into the street; it moved across the empty beds, stiff sheets shivering, and past the peeling teal paint of the swinging doors; Xiao Lin prepared for a last stout push while her son's cry and the echoes of it multiplied in a terrible, monstrous din.

The doors of the delivery room erupted. Singed clothes, sooty hair, mad eyes, shaking, flinging arms pushed through the doors in a great mass of shouts. Bodies were deposited, lain quickly, gently, trembling, jerking onto the empty beds and the floor between them; white sheets softened, blooming with blood. In the hallways, in each previously empty room of the hospital, Feng's first cry was drowned out. Xiao Lin opened her eyes with a great swallow of air. She saw: first, Wei's face above her, staring fanatically at the doctor; then, the doctor, his blue gloved hands between her legs, his blanched face turned toward the door; and finally, the terrible picture. Frozen faces of young men and women—other people's children—had invaded the peace of her room, carried in on makeshift stretchers, limp between sagging arms. A young man her little brother's age stood by the bed to her left. He was looking at her, a glaze over his eyes, his mouth slightly open, and for a fraction of a second, before she saw his hands, slick and shining red, she was appalled by her naked open legs. She breathed—the rank smell of sweat and blood—gulped down the acid that rose to her throat, turned her head to the wall and closed her eyes.

It was her prerogative not to look. She was having a child. She had no duty, not now, not to these others. She tried to conjure Robert Redford, the graceful lines of his body as he stood beside that car, the carefree yellow of it. She focused on the black doors of her eyelids; she gave her final push. She did not open her eyes again until she felt a hand on her arm and the sweet salty breath of her son on her face. There he was, looking at her with bright, dark eyes. She held him against her chest. The poor boy, he had stopped crying. Intimidated by the chorus that had risen to accompany him, he closed his mouth, and, nudging at his mother's breast, didn't make a single sound.

On the television screen, the day after Feng's birth, the counter-revolutionaries were tracked down and brought to justice; young men in gray-blue shirts were apprehended, hands cuffed, heads forced down and paraded before the camera; crisply narrated montages played to the monotone of hollow-faced confessions. A few months after Xiao Lin took Feng home from the hospital, this blitz of media coverage was replaced by a rolling green field. Peasants dotted the field, their backs bent. Rice production had risen in Shenzhen, the weather was 26C and sunny. Like changing a tape in the VCR, normalcy had been restored.

Xiao Lin took this as permission to forget. She had spent the first weeks of Feng's life examining him for defects, worrying over each spot on his skin, each cough-like burp. But he was perfect, a beauty with fat pink cheeks, big black eyes and smooth, smooth skin. He was healthy and active; his favorite activity was rolling over, in a sudden lurch, onto his stomach. The only odd thing was that he hardly cried, but this, her husband convinced her, was not a bad thing at all. Unlike most new parents, they slept full nights. What good luck! What assurance, that bending her head down and excusing herself had been the right thing to do after all.

Feng's affliction would not begin to show for another half a year. At ten months and two weeks, when the white ridges of sharp new baby teeth pushed up from the pink earth of his gums, a strange rash appeared on his fingers, and Feng began to bawl. Xiao Lin and Da Ping had just left for work. Wei, washing a batch of dirty diapers, rinsed off her arms and ran to the boy. He was thrashing, twitching to one side and then the other and crying like he had never cried before. Wei picked him up and held him tightly—he squirmed as if trying to fall out of her arms—she cooed and bounced and fed him his milk until he quieted. Strange, but Wei didn't think too much of it. After all, that was what her own children had been like, waking up cranky and crying for food. If anything, Feng was becoming more typical. She laid him back on the bed and was about to return to her washing when she saw his hands. They were balled up in little fists, and around the knuckles and fingertips were small red spots, sores scattered here and there.

Wei scooped him up immediately and took him to the hospital. There were a number of possible causes for infant skin afflictions—bug bites, allergic reactions, heat rash, eczema, infant acne—she took home a tube of ointments for each, and applied two, one on each hand. By the end of the day the sores appeared to have shrunk, and so when Xiao Lin and Da Ping came home there was not much fuss. But the marks persisted. When the first spots disappeared, new ones came. They grew larger and more inflamed. They appeared around his lips. By his first birthday, they had spread to Feng's wrists and the backs of his hands. Xiao Lin began to have nightmares, visions that woke her in the middle of the night, though she could never remember what they were.

One night two months into the ordeal, Xiao Lin snapped awake from one of these—a slippery, red flash—to find Feng howling and thrashing beside her. Da Ping was already awake, trying to calm the child and prodding Xiao Lin. Wei ran into the room and turned on the light.

One of the sores had broken open, by the base of Feng's right hand thumb, and blood was gushing out of it, a thin red streak running down his hand and dripping onto the bed sheets. Xiao Lin screamed. She stood up and stepped back. What she saw was not her son. What she saw was the young man by her birthing bed, and his hands—bloody, shining, frozen before his chest. Her last sight before Feng was born.

Three months of Robert Redford, undone by this. If only she had known—if only she had read the signs, if only Feng had been born one day, one minute earlier. Was that what her body had been telling her, with those false contractions? She would have jumped up and down to break her water sooner, she would have followed the pain, screamed to make it bigger, pushed harder, begged the doctors for medications to speed it up, she would have cut herself open to bring him into the world before that dreadful night.

Feng howled louder. He jerked his good hand to his mouth, put his fingers inside it like any babe would to comfort itself, and sucked ferociously. His eyes were open, large, black, bright, terrified. He opened his mouth and his hand came out. Xiao Lin screamed again and backed against the wall. The hand was covered with blood. The wet hole of his mouth, his tiny shards of teeth, were bright red. Wei moved Feng's other hand away from his scrunched face. "Oh Lu Xun," she said as she picked him up, pressing his bloody hands into her night shirt, "Here's your little cannibal." Xiao Lin sank to the floor. So this—this was the punishment for witnessing.

The boy was biting himself, and the hospital had no explanation, though not for lack of trying. Blood was drawn, spit swabbed, pulse taken, weight, height, blood pressure, temperature, urine samples, stool samples, tests run and repeated, textbooks consulted, experts phoned. Nothing, apparently, was wrong. The only number that was a little off was his uric acid. Like an old man's, the levels were a bit high. What did this mean? Not much, as far as they could tell.

Feng's hands were bandaged, his arms wrapped tightly at his sides with a swaddling blanket. It was suggested that his teeth be pulled. Xiao Lin, white-faced and faint, with not much more than vanity to cling onto, refused to have a toothless child. They settled on a temporary solution—to protect his hands with tiny mittens, his first in a long line of hand wear. To protect the tongue and lips a permanent pacifier was stuffed into his mouth, tied around his head with a strip of cloth. As they left the hospital, Feng bundled tight like a silkworm, Wei shook her head. Impossible, she said, impossible. How could they not have a solution?

Wei did not rest. She combed through medical textbooks and carried Feng to every hospital in Beijing, encountering an endless string of shaking heads, of "I've never seen anything like it." Xiao Lin stopped going to work. Da Ping's refrigerator business was flourishing, and at a time when no one was in the mood to celebrate, the family was quietly amassing wealth. A thick, torpid silence sunk into the walls of the apartment, broken only by Feng's screams.

It was the middle of the day, a month after the hospital had failed, when Xiao Lin received the call. Wei was out, somewhere. Wei was always out, the only one still feverishly hopeful, and Xiao Lin, who could not help but feel exhausted whenever she saw her mother-in-law, was thankful for this. Xiao Lin sat and looked silently at her son, his skin plump and pink and smooth, but all of it bound up by what might as well have been a rope. Xiao Lin hadn't eaten anything. She needed to use the toilet but the thought of standing up, getting out of her chair, was overwhelming. Feng was sleeping, the pacifier in his mouth. Once in a while he coughed and spat the thing out, and Xiao Lin's arm would dart out to replace it; otherwise she did not move. The mittens, the pacifier—it was all almost laughable. When the phone rang, she sighed. "Yes."

"Hello, you are the family with the self-biting boy?" a woman said.

The woman spoke with a strange accent. Xiao Lin could not place it. "Who is this?"

"I am . . . a doctor for children. There is a self-biting boy in the household? Yes?"

"How—"

"Somebody called and spoke with the assistant. The grandmother of the boy? Yes?"

"The grandmother."

But before she could think anything more, something inside Xiao Lin cracked. She began to speak, hands shaking, eyes fixed on Feng, who in sleep was the closest to what she had imagined a son would be. Feng's symptoms, the precautionary measures, his teeth, his heat rash from being over-swaddled, his mittens, the endless tests, how he howled when they stuck him with needles, how he spat and shuddered, the night they had all woken up. She talked backwards, from now to the time of the hands and the hospital's utter uselessness, plastic tubes filled with blood in vain, to the perfect days when he was a good natured beautiful baby who never cried, when his sudden movements were surprises—she talked all the way back until she reached the birth. She stopped.

"Do you know what he has?" she said.

"Yes, yes, please bring him over," the doctor said. "As soon as possible, preferably. We will see him." A pause. "We have seen many cases like his, unfortunately."

2.

Xiao Lin arrived in Tokyo at night and even from the plane the city had been aglow. In Shinjuku the buildings were lit up with bright signs in violet and blue and green, the streets illuminated with functioning lamps. No one spat on the sidewalks or threw their trash on the ground. Cars took up more lanes than bicycles. The bicycles looked slimmer too, their metal sleek and light, free of rust. The anxieties that kept her awake on the plane dissipated into the wide, swept street and the clean uncrumbling corners of sidewalks—it no longer felt impulsive to have gone immediately to the travel agency and purchased a flight for herself and Feng after hanging up with the doctor. The things her mother and sister had said about the Japanese being barbarians, not to be trusted with Chinese flesh, were no longer relevant. Lu Xun had studied medicine in Japan, Wei said. Wei was right. Japan was the future.

The clinic was on a residential street lined with ginkgoes, a gray brick building that, if not for the placard and intercom at the gate, Xiao Lin would have mistaken for a large apartment complex. She could not read the sign, but she checked the building number against what she'd written and, holding Feng tight against her chest with one hand, lightly pressed the buzzer. After a few moments, a nurse in white scrubs emerged from the door and opened the gate. The nurse motioned silently for Xiao Lin to follow.

The inside of the clinic was much larger than it had appeared from the street. It did not smell like hospital, the sharp acid of sterilized instruments, but was perfectly odorless. The floors and walls were white, and there were many windows. Surfaces that were not white were made of glass. Xiao Lin walked lightly, suddenly conscious of how dirty the bottoms of her shoes must be. She was led up an elevator (an elevator!) to the top floor, where skylights flooded the hall with natural light. Through the windows on her left was a rooftop garden. The nurse knocked on a door and opened it. Xiao Lin stepped inside.

At a desk, her back to Xiao Lin, a woman with short white hair tapped at a machine that looked like a television, a beeping and sighing contraption that Xiao Lin had never seen before. The wall she faced was made entirely of glass and looked out on the skyscrapers of downtown Tokyo; the woman sat, perched at the edge of a tall chair like a hawk preparing to dive off for a hunt. The woman turned around and faced Xiao Lin. She was much younger than her white hair indicated— thirty, at most forty years old. She wore a white lab coat over white slacks and a fitted white tee. Her eyes were stone gray. She handed Xiao Lin a business card, one side in Chinese and the other in English:

Maya Takaomi, MD, PhD
The Center for Abnormal Behavior in Children

"Please sit," Dr. Takaomi said. She smiled. "We will communicate in Chinese?"

Xiao Lin nodded and sat.

"I'll have a look at the boy?" Dr. Takaomi stood up and pulled a small examining table from the wall. The table was cushioned with soft blankets and had protective rails that snapped up from the sides. She took Feng and placed him on the table.

Dr. Takaomi was remarkably small, almost child-sized, yet she carried in her stiff-shouldered stance a manner of utter authority. She unwrapped the blanket around Feng. Immediately he began to squirm. One hand holding him still, she pulled a light from the wall, looked into his eyes and ears and mouth, put up one finger and moved it from side to side across his face. She lightly poked various parts of his body with a toothpick. He began to cry. She examined his hands. She picked up the boy, holding him out at arms length. He stilled and looked at the doctor.

"Yes," she finally said.

"Yes?"

"Yes, I am afraid he has it."

"Has what? What does he have?"

Silence.

"How do you know?"

"Well, for one, his eyes."

Dr. Takaomi wrapped Feng back up in the swaddling blanket. "Of course we will have to run the tests," she said. "But based on what you've said and an initial examination, I don't see what else it could be."

She gave Feng back to Xiao Lin and folded the table up into the wall. Xiao Lin looked at her son's eyes. Dr. Takaomi turned to her television-like machine, where she began again to poke at a slab of buttons. The clicking and tapping made Xiao Lin look up. Japanese words were appearing on the screen as the doctor tapped. Xiao Lin had seen a similar machine, though bigger and uglier, in her boss's office, but she had never seen anyone use it..

"Is that—"

"Ah, how do you say in Chinese—an electronic head, I believe. It is a very smart machine, yes. We have many smart machines here, you'll see."

Dr. Takaomi placed her hand on a small oval contraption connected to the electronic head with a cord, tapped once, and on the screen there appeared an odd drawing of the letter X that looked like two worms knotted together. She closed her eyes and breathed.

There was something about the doctor that made the room feel as if it were tilting from side to side. It seemed to Xiao Lin that Dr. Takaomi knew everything—everything about Feng, but also everything about Xiao Lin. Perhaps it was her hair, short and white and standing on end as if electric, yet very neat. Or perhaps it was the way she spoke, with a slight twinkle in her voice, so that even as she consoled and said a thing that was deeply empathetic she seemed to hide an excitement.

"Yes, back to business," she said. "I'm afraid you will not be pleased with what you will hear. I will continue?"

Xiao Lin held Feng against her chest, bouncing with her hand behind his head to quiet his little murmurs. She nodded.

"It is an X-linked recessive mutation," Dr. Takaomi said. "One in five hundred thousand boys. Your son is very special indeed."

"Unfortunately, one of the genes you contributed to your son contained a misspelling. Unfortunately, one is all it takes. He is unable to recycle his DNA, and as a result he has excess uric acid and exhibits this self-abusing behavior, though it is still unclear how the behavioral aspects are linked to the physiology. But his symptoms are currently mild, yes? At two or three years he will learn his strength. He may bite off whole fingers and chew off whole lips. He may thrash so hard he breaks his neck."

Dr. Takaomi tapped the electronic head.

"You may be thinking, does he feel pain? The answer is yes. He feels it as strongly as you and I. He does not desire pain. However, he cannot control himself. Inside his body is a code—an instruction sheet, yes? It tells him to destroy. If he survives to full consciousness and develops complex emotions, he will be tormented by this part he cannot control. The good news is that the *imp of the perverse*—that is just a name I like to call it, not a medical term, Ms. Lin—is not always active. The destructive action itself takes only a matter of minutes, you see, sometimes even seconds. The bad news is, no one can know when the imp will take over, not even himself."

A whistling gasp escaped from Xiao Lin's throat. When Dr. Takaomi said the words *imp of the perverse,* the ducts beneath her eyes that she'd dammed up after the first night she woke up to the bloody scream broke. Tears flowed freely, dropping onto Feng's head. Dr. Takaomi paused, opened her mouth as if to say something, then turned to the electronic head, letting out a long breath. She clicked on it again, and a photo of a five- or six-year-old boy filled the screen. The boy's face was scarred with scratch marks, craters and grooves and dashes, and in the place where his nose should have been there was a gaping black hole.

"Here is a boy whose fingers went up his nostrils and annihilated his sinus cartilage from the inside."

She clicked the screen, and another photo appeared. It showed a young man with no lips and only one eye who sat in a wheelchair, his body bent in sharp angles.

"This boy bit off his lips. He has also removed one eye. He could have done it with a pencil or with a spoon. He could have done it with his fingers."

She clicked again. A close-up shot of a red, swollen arm with small black holes puncturing the entire length. Three of five fingers on the hand were gone.

"Biting of the fingers is most common. The holes were made from a fork."

Another boy without a nose, his arm in a sling. Mutilated hand after mutilated hand, stumps where fingers should have been. A finger that still had its tip but was missing a chunk at the knuckle so large that the bone was visible. And so on. Scarred flesh, missing eyes, ears, noses, teeth, fingers, toes. Boys in wheelchairs with their necks in traction and arms splinted, tied to wooden planks.

"Most boys will find some way to die before they reach puberty. Often, puberty itself is delayed. Very lucky boys will survive to thirty, perhaps even forty. There is a spectrum between mild and severe, yes? In all cases, however, the life will be a half-life. The boy will always require care and supervision."

The final picture was of a young boy, perhaps four or five years old, with no teeth and half of his lip chewed off. Dr. Takaomi covered the bottom half of the face, so that only the boy's eyes were visible. They were black and bright and stared straight into the camera.

"We are told that the boys will also be fools. But I do not believe it. The boys are remarkably attuned emotionally. And how can he learn if when he looks at a book, his hands automatically tear the pages out, if he is given a pencil and stabs his arm? Look at these eyes," she said. "How intelligent and searching they are."

Xiao Lin did not yet understand that it was not her fault, that her son's affliction had started decades before she even knew her husband's name. She did not understand what a gene was, or a mutation, or all the English letters that spelled out words she didn't know, DNA and RNA and HPRT. What she heard was that one little thing had caused all this, one misstep, and when Dr. Takaomi explained that DNA was the material that made a person what they would become, she imagined a clear thin tissue covering Feng's heart, twisting and breaking at the moment of his birth. *Unfortunately, one is all it takes.*

And when, after samples were taken from Feng and sent to the laboratory for genetic testing, Dr. Takaomi gave Xiao Lin a tour of the clinic, the sparkling cafeteria where fresh vitamin-fortified food was prepared and served, the inpatient living quarters immaculately safe with soft corners and pillowed walls, the garden where the children played under expert supervision, Xiao Lin saw all the things she had failed to do for her son. In the center the doctor kept rooms for about thirty children with severe life-impeding abnormalities. She had seen a handful of patients with Feng's problem, and published papers on the topic. Many of her patients were Japanese and East Asian, but there were children from all over the world too, including one Russian boy living inpatient who was very much like Feng.

At the first floor Dr. Takaomi led them into a long hallway, its walls padded with white cushions. At the end of the hallway was what looked like a small playroom. It was mostly white, but had dots of color: picture books on low shelves, crayons and paints, and soft, pillowy blocks. Ten or so children were inside. A girl ran around an orange rug in circles. A boy at the table was drawing slowly, creating a spread of papers all decorated with the SONY logo in various sizes and colors. The girl across from him ripped colored paper methodically into smaller and smaller squares. Another boy was sitting with a nurse and throwing a small ball ferociously into a strangely shaped box that seemed to be designed to keep the ball from ricocheting out. They were children, but their faces were distorted, some too big for how old they seemed to be, some with thin slanted eyes and some with elongated foreheads or crooked jaws. Xiao Lin felt a twinge of involuntary revulsion and pulled Feng closer to her chest, as if to assure him that he was not like them. Then she saw the brown-haired boy in the corner. He was attended to by two nurses in white and had a padded stick across his shoulders, to which his arms had been bound with white cloth so that he looked like a scarecrow, and he was staring straight at Xiao Lin. When she moved closer she saw he was tied to his chair. The nurses next to him were reading him a book, but he did not pay attention. He looked at Xiao Lin, his eyes sharp as if trying to pierce into the core of her bones. Dr. Takaomi walked over.

"This is Viktor, the boy I spoke of?" she said to Xiao Lin. To the boy she said something in Russian.

Viktor, eyes still on Xiao Lin, began to shout at her in Russian, spitting and hollering, grimacing and struggling with the ropes that were tying him up. Xiao Lin stepped back.

"What is he saying?"

"Oh, nothing," Dr. Takaomi said. "He likes you. He's hostile because he can see that you've been crying. It's self-sabotage. Do you understand?"

Xiao Lin tried her best to smile at Viktor.

"Viktor's parents have not yet come around," Dr. Takaomi said when they left the room. They walked back down the hall. "But I think it will be only a matter of time."

"What do you mean?"

"You see, the syndrome was discovered some twenty or thirty years ago by a pair of Americans, but the Americans haven't discovered a way to cure it."

She stopped before the elevator and looked at Xiao Lin, her eyes gleaming.

"You could also say that the Americans, like Viktor's parents, have not yet found their courage."

The doors dinged open and Dr. Takaomi stepped inside. "Do you know where your courage is, Ms. Lin?"

It was not a choice. Xiao Lin closed her eyes and let her picture of motherhood fall away. There would be no smiling baby, crawling then standing then toddling, no red-scarfed schoolboy running home with his backpack, no teenager studying ascetically for exams. Wheelchairs, gauze, a scarecrow frame. Angry, terrified eyes. Between this and Dr. Takaomi's cure, there was no choice at all.

The deep brain stimulation procedure that Dr. Takaomi had adapted for boys like Feng had already been successfully implemented on patients with Parkinson's disease. The doctor herself had installed what she called the "brain pacemaker device" on three separate cases of the syndrome, and two of three had responded with miraculous results. Their self-injurious behavior had completely ceased. They were as close to normal as they could be, having lived already a good span of their lives with the disease. The operation had never been attempted on a boy as young as Feng, mostly because a case had never reached her so early. It was possible, she was willing to bet, that if treated now the boy could have an entirely "normal" life. Complications were possible too, of course, but how could they be worse than what was already in store? It was not a procedure that was widespread or well-known, no, but of course the disease itself was not widespread or well-known.

The pacemaker would send periodic electric pulses to his brain, keep the imp in check. Because nothing like this had ever been done before, Feng would stay at the Center for some time, at least until the age of five. At the Center they would monitor his progress and also educate him, socialize him against his impulses with the curricula they had developed for these boys.

The specifics of the operation were terrifying. Xiao Lin pushed them out of her mind. She did not want to imagine her son, her Feng, his scalp lifted and a hole cut in his skull. She could not think of what it would mean, that wires would be eased inside until they prodded a little globe at the bottom of his brain, the wires then threaded down his neck and attached to a titanium battery disc that would be folded under the skin of his chest, directly mirroring his heart. After the operation was done, the mechanism would be invisible to the naked eye, save for a few thin surgical scars. That was the image Xiao Lin focused on as she signed the consent papers, as she held the results of the confirmatory test. Her son sewn up and returned to her—her living, breathing son, to the naked eye no different from anyone else.

County Maps

Joe Worthen

University of North Carolina Wilmington; MFA

Suzanne stands framed by the open door with August behind her and her bike too, laid like who gives a shit in the weeds, one wheel spinning. A backpack hangs off her left shoulder. Binoculars hang off her neck. Suzanne has a shirt with a picture of the Grand Canyon on over a bathing suit top. And she's got on some denim shorts tapering to white knots like Spanish moss. Suzanne has got hair with a long wave in it and bangs that are sort of fucked up because she cut them herself in the back of a Silverado that was moving at the time.

Jack squints dim eyes at her through his bonfire hangover. Jack is like what do you want? What are you doing here at the house of my dad with so much ambient purpose? Jack has got a robin tattooed in dark ink on his shoulder and varsity muscle cut down to camouflage boxers. Suzanne walks past him into the house.

She sits across a low mahogany table from Jack, who is eating Corn Pops. The wall behind Suzanne is covered with mounted deer heads. One for every year, starting with 1985 and going straight through now, lined up chronologically like a one sign zodiac. All the deer are gray. None of the deer are brown or tan. All the deer are gray like lint.

Suzanne says, "You remember what we talked about last night?" Jack remembers her face through wood smoke. Jack remembers her pale shape naked on the corner of his bed, tuning his guitar and talking. And then, yeah, Jack remembers what they talked about last night.

"The maps," Jack says.

"That's right," says Suzanne, who has mapped this whole county, the woods, the pastures, the farms, the strip malls. Every foot of the county accounted for except the island, which she's been coming to all along. The island doesn't appear on most existing cartography and when it does it's just an unnamed shape in a named river. This is the same island that Jack's family has been illegally hunting on for a couple generations. The same island that Jack offered, in one of the sweet moments before sleep where compromise is infinite, to guide Suzanne across.

"The island's full of trash, you really want to go out there?" he asks her.

"I do," Suzanne says.

"Today might not be the best day," Jack says, eyes drifting from deer to deer.

"Look Jack, I'm going one way or the other." Suzanne stands up. "I made you a turkey sandwich but I can eat two."

"Is that right?" Jack asks. "You packed a sandwich for me?" Suzanne nods. "I only have been out there a couple times." Suzanne edges out from behind the table. Jack runs his right hand down his face, drains the milk from his bowl and says, "Let me get dressed."

Suzanne and Jack travel by bike to a gravel parking lot off state highway 107. The neighborhood kids follow them at a distance, some of them threading whispers through street noise, some of them quiet. The kids follow Suzanne and Jack from the gravel lot, over pine needles and beer cans to the river where Jack is already wading in like lets get this over with and Suzanne pulls her Grand Canyon t-shirt off like a plastic wrapper, and stashes it in her bag. Then Suzanne and Jack are both in deep, wading towards the other side, where the last piece of the county is.

Halfway out into the river Suzanne looks back with water up to her shoulders, the bottom fringe of hair wet, her backpack held overhead. Neighborhood kids watch from the shore, some under cypress branches, some in the shadow of the overpass, all ankle-deep in mud, knee-deep in reeds. She moves, blurred by nascent morning heat, leading a slow wake until she reaches the opposite bank, steepened from current and latticed with roots. She climbs from the river. She hops something low, barbwire. Then a car comes by on the highway, a quick blur of noise, and Suzanne disappears into private property with Jack just behind her.

A mottled sunlight covers Suzanne like snakeskin. Suzanne hits a sequence of buttons on the handheld with dirty fingers and a satellite gives her coordinates. As she walks, numbers spool out, measurements, racing and pausing with the reception.

"What's this one?" Jack points to a number.

"Distance."

"What's this one?"

"Altitude."

"County's flat as a tabletop," Jack says wiping river water off his forehead with his own wadded shirt. Jack leads Suzanne around the perimeter, climbing over root systems and kicking soda bottles. Every time he glances at the sun his hangover folds over on itself. And the heat comes at them both in long numb waves.

"At least talk to me or something," Jack says.

"All right," Suzanne says as she marks another square of graph paper with a small line. "Are you interested at all in cartography?"

"Did I say I was last night?"

"Yeah."

"I'm not uninterested." Jack shrugs. He leads Suzanne around a small inlet humming with mosquitoes and damselflies.

"You didn't have to come out here just because I fucked you," Suzanne says.

"Maybe you could tell me some of what you're doing," Jack says. The back of his eyes throb and his stomach is raw.

"I'm just making preliminary renderings using the data from the GPS. And taking notes, marking coordinates."

"This ain't gonna be the real map?"

"No Jack. Look." Suzanne stops and holds her pad out in front of her, slight pencil marks on a blue grid, nothing but a thin outline moving around the island. "Just a sketch."

"So what then?" Jack slaps a mosquito on his forearm. Suzanne slaps a mosquito on her neck.

"I take the draft home and do the final map in ink."

"You got the whole county done like you said?"

"Except this yeah," and she starts moving again and so do the numbers on the GPS, climbing inches towards feet toward miles and miles.

They find an old motorboat flipped between two cypress trees, covered in algae. Jack walks out on it and smokes a cigarette. Suzanne looks at the shape of him and chews the edge of her pencil. The taste of wood and paint with Jack there, deep summer tan, facing out at the river, the topography of his back laid bare, which, similar to the county itself, isn't simply flat. When Jack turns back toward her he sees something, puts his finger over his mouth like be quiet and points behind Suzanne. Three gray deer, two small, and one big, move through the black gum deeper in the island, totally silent, then gone. Jack jumps off the boat.

"They're the pale ones from your deer room," Suzanne says.

"Yeah the ones you find out here are like that. They're gray and a little smaller than you get other side of the river."

"You ever kill one?"

"Nah," Jack says. "My brothers each got a couple and my dad's got a bunch. But, I don't know, they're quick." Jack puts his cigarette out between his bare foot and the dirt.

"Don't know how you smoke hungover," Suzanne says.

"I'm sort of hungry," Jack says. Suzanne rations out the two turkey sandwiches she has in her bag. Jack eats his in three bites, wedging the white bread into his cheeks, across his crouched tongue. After, he draws a line in the soil with his toe and says, "I am exactly as hungry as I was before." Suzanne doesn't say anything, just negotiates her own bites until her sandwich is gone too. "Are you sure there was even turkey on that? It tasted like a bread sandwich. You should use more turkey. Just putting one slice of turkey on a sandwich is more of a waste than using too much because with one you can't even tell it's there. You know what I mean? That turkey was imperceptible."

"All right, shut up." Suzanne spits and keeps on.

At 7 mi they find the place where they started. Suzanne makes a note on her drawing and says, for Jack's benefit, "This island is seven miles around."

"That all you need?" Jack asks, looking at the distant overpass or the shadow directly below it. Jack is feeling better; he takes a drag from his flask, silver and dented. Jack hopes maybe Suzanne will want to keep walking.

"It's just noon, lets take some passes across the interior," Suzanne says.

"You want any?" Jack holds the flask out to her.

"Nah," Suzanne says. She and Jack start toward the interior of the island. They move through the black gum and oak, occasional sheets of rusted metal bent and half-buried. At 1.6 mi they find a steel drum filled with old cell phones, some whole, some crushed down to black plastic scrap, light as paper in Suzanne's cupped hand. Jack sorts some whole phones out from the rest, wonders about resale value. Suzanne doesn't pause for long, keeps measuring the width of the island by walking it. At 2 mi they find a shattered toilet. At 2.8 mi they find a tree, struck by lightning that the both of them had probably seen flash sometime in the last year. The tree is curled against the summer sky like an antler, bleached white and dead.

"How'd you think to map the county Suzy?" Jack asks, looking up the tree.

"Only way to know the whole place."

"You map the quarry?"

"Yeah."

"You went down in the caves?"

"Yeah."

"You map all the strip malls? You get both McDonalds?"

"Yep."

"You get the Illusions Smoke Shop up there by the county line?" Jack asks.

"Yes I did, Jack. I got it all."

At 3.3 mi they come across a burned down house, mostly collapsed except on one side. "Huh," Suzanne says looking across the small clearing to the lopsided thing. "Unanticipated domicile."

Jack looks at Suzanne's ass and tries to remember more about the sex than just blurred out bodies, like some skin channel only coming through halfway.

"You know anything about this Jack?"

"Yeah, long time ago some people lived out here. Then the house caught fire and they left. Dad said they moved south but they still own the land here," Jack says.

Suzanne and Jack approach the house, over fragments of it, charred and scattered in tall grass as if it's is slowly expanding outward. Closer, they can see that ivy has climbed over the front and up and out of a jagged black hole in the roof. Jack tries the door, which is open, and crosses the dim threshold with Suzanne just behind him. Inside is cool and just moving through the space stirs dust into the sunlight in cauliflower plumes. To the left is the burned part, totally fallen in, and to the right is a kitchen. All the drawers are pulled out, all the silverware and broken china is on the floor in an even layer. The windows are all shattered and there's honeysuckle blooming in the sink.

"Why do you think the fire stopped here?" Suzanne asks, glancing at what was destroyed.

"Heard it was rain."

"Yeah?"

"Yeah, a storm came in and stopped the fire is what my dad said."

They walk into a hall behind the kitchen, which turns black and caves in almost right away. But there's a door first that leads to a bedroom with all its wallpaper peeling in curls and glass and manila folders all over the ground. And there's nothing else but a bare single mattress, crooked, in the center of the space.

Suzanne checks her handheld. The numbers on it jump at random, severed from the satellites by maybe something in the roof, distance and altitude now in flux. Jack comes close behind Suzanne and puts his hand on the slope of her hip, turns her toward him and gives her a kiss with rye whiskey in it. Suzanne kisses him back, runs her hands up the front of his chest. Jack takes her Grand Canyon t-shirt off and tosses it, sets more dust off. The numbers are racing from 0 to 9 and back, over and over. Suzanne's got his jeans off, pulling him down. Jack's got a couple fingers in her, thinking that this is maybe easier than remembering. Suzanne's got nothing but an anklet on. Jack's sprawled on the mattress; Suzanne's on top of him, teeth clenched, moving back and forth, dust on new sweat. And it doesn't take more than a couple minutes for Suzanne to finish silent, ragged nails pulling blood out of Jack's shoulder, and Jack, seconds later, with a short dense sound.

Jack picks some loose pieces of glass out of his back and Suzanne takes a drink from his flask, leans on the window frame, one leg slick, trying to get a breath of cool air with no luck.

This is just about the middle of the island, she thinks. This is just about the farthest you can get from the county without leaving. Outside, between some pine trees, the gray deer move. They're moving slow, about the speed of clouds, and she thinks, how hard could it possibly be to shoot one of those things? Maybe Jack just isn't the sort to kill. Suzanne wonders what happens to people like that.

She turns back to Jack who is looking at her with a sort of dazed interest; dirt swirled in patterns over his body, naked as the mattress.

"What?" she asks him.

"Just weird. Been to school together for like ten years and don't know shit about you. You're over off 107 right?"

"That's right."

"Never seen your people around, you know?"

"Live with my grandma, Jack. She only gets off the couch when she needs to defrost something in the microwave."

"Didn't your dad—" Jack thinks he remembers a rumor, one strand of yearbook gossip, then thinks twice about it. Suzanne ties her bathing suit top back on.

"Didn't he what?"

"Have a drunk driving accident a couple years back?"

"No. My dad drowned in the parking lot at the Texas Steakhouse. He drowned in this much water." She stretches her thumb and forefinger just enough to show that they could contain the measure. "Just a big shallow puddle. Took up the whole front lot, ran into mud and grass at the edges then down the other way to near the traffic light. Rain black, little gasoline rainbows around his fingertips. He was walking back from somewhere. Passed out drunk. They found him in the morning in that still water with the neon Texas hanging in the fog like a star sign."

"Sorry," Jack looks away.

"I didn't ever speak to the man, Jack." Suzanne tosses him his flask.

Jack holds the flask in front of his chest, thinks about it and says, "Shit. Figures you'd want to get out of this place, instead of trying to know it better."

Suzanne, a constellation of nettles in her hair, nods her head like yeah, like I see your point. Then she draws a quick rectangle on her graph paper, writes a couple words, and they step out into the early afternoon to map the rest of the county.

The Turk

Andrew MacDonald
University of Massachusetts Amherst; MFA

Today I drink coffee on the terrace outside of Café de la Régence, in Paris. Across from me, there are a series of tables set up for an amateur chess tournament. For some reason, they're playing outdoors, the playing area partitioned off with a thick velvet rope. Overhead, the sky resembles light-blue pastels smudged by the thumb. The players are largely clumsy. One of my students, Jacques Dieppe, is playing against another boy; from my vantage point, with the help of a lens, I can see that Dieppe is crushing his opponent with impunity.

I am in love with Dieppe's sister, whom I also tutor, but who has no desire to become better. She stands just beyond the velvet rope, in a yellow dress of such extravagant pleating that it would take hours to count the folds. Once her brother has won, she waves to me and I wave back. She walks over to my table. Without asking, she takes my coffee and drinks the remainder of it. The foam from the milk leaves a line of white under her nose.

She sets it down and starts pulling me up by the shoulder. "Come on, Jacques wants you to see the board before they clear it." And before I can protest she's practically carrying me to the velvet rope. I barely have time to snatch my walking stick.

Dieppe stands on the other side of the rope and claps me on the shoulder. He's a full head taller than me, dressed quite regally, though some sweat has matted his shirt, and the force of his slap nearly puts me to my knees. "He never saw the end coming," he says. I tell him he used the French Defense marvellously.

The table shows that his opponent either suffers from some sort of debilitating mental condition, or that he's played chess only a few times in his life. This is Jacques's second win out of some twenty matches he's played at the Régence.

"Got a bit out of control at the end, though, didn't I," he says, and laughs, and exchanges kisses with his sister, whose neck has a single vein running up it, almost rudely, that disappears under her collarbone and beneath her dress.

Over the span of three years, I played the finest chess players the world has ever seen. I battled François-André Danican Philidor, widely considered the best chess player in Europe. That match took place in Paris, in 1783, in the presence of many members of the French Academy of Sciences; his son, noting Philidor's exhaustion, declared that nobody had fatigued his father to such an extent.

Prior to that I played the duc de Bouillan, Benjamin Franklin, and for Emperor Joseph II, who had me play during a state visit from the Grand Duke Paul of Russia. It was during this visit to Schönbrunn palace that I fell in love with Paul's wife Maria Feodorovna, the duchess, and I maintain that she fell in love with me.

I am to history as air is to lungs: breathed in by many, remembered by none. I have never entered a formal tournament in my life. Aside from occasionally being cited as the tutor of the lower aristocracy, a source of income for most of my life, my name appears nowhere in the game's literature.

For three years, I operated a machine that might strike a chord in your memory, a chess-playing automaton constructed in the appearance of a mystical oriental. My employer was a Hungarian named Kempelen, the machine's inventor. You can find a book that answers questions about the Turk's age, marital status, and some amusing, if ridiculous, anecdotes about its life.

I've never read the book personally, but since I operated the Turk for much of its European tour, I am nearly positive that the book has nothing to do with me or my life, and is therefore erroneous, in need of correction.

I only own one proper formal suit and the last time I wore it predates my tutoring of Jacques. The fabric itches around my neck, and, looking in the mirror, I see what I've been hiding under my beard for so many years: a terrain of thick chasmic lines, a particularly offensive pair bookending my lips and running right up to my nose. Some irregularities of the skin make my cheeks look rough and dry. A scar runs just along the underside of my chin, its origins a mystery to me.

There is incongruity when I look at my reflection, as if someone had taken a mallet to the glass and fractured it into three: there is me, now; there is me, when younger; there is the Turk, who has by now become such a part of me that to peel it from me would be like peeling living meat from bone.

The time is five o'clock. The Dieppes are expecting me at their home in one hour. The invitation was written by one of the Dieppe's servants, though when I run my fingers across the letters, I imagine that Clara Dieppe's hands had guided the nib of her pen.

I have played Clara six times since I began tutoring her brother. Unlike Jacques, who idolizes the French masters and their almost cold approach to the game, Clara acts rashly, attempting attacks that betray an almost psychotic willingness to suffer grave injury to inflict pain on another.

"Ah," she'll say, taking my rook at the cost of her queen, a ludicrous trade. "What do you think about that?"

I make it a point not to say much to her, or anyone, since my voice is ugly, gravel rubbing against gravel, but sometimes I'll mutter, "Impulsive," or, "Not bad," though it doesn't matter whether I encourage her or offer critique. She continues to sacrifice her small army with sadistic pleasure.

Also: she refuses to play as black. I've spent an embarrassing amount of my days trying to decipher what that means.

A brief description of the Turk. Kempelen told me he had constructed the machine after seeing the illusionist François Pelletier perform at Schönbrunn Palace. The Turk earned Kempelen the patronage of Maria Theresa.

The Turk had a life-sized head and torso, brown eyes, a neatly-coiffed black moustache. Atop the head, a turban held together by a single jewel. In one hand, the Turk held a pipe, while its other arm directed traffic on the chessboard in front of it. The torso sat in a large cabinet, which stretched four feet by two and a half feet, with a height of three feet. When I sat inside the cabinet, I felt like I'd been encased in amber.

Embedded in the cabinet, a system of magnets by which I could discern my opponent's moves and a mechanism that controlled the Turk's arm. I could also communicate with Kempelen via a series of numbers, grafted on metal discs, which I could turn to spell out my messages in code without anyone noticing.

"What do you think?" Kempelen asked, following his proposal. We were in his workshop. I went into the Turk, out of the Turk. I told him a price, and he countered it with a slightly lower figure, which I accepted.

After spending one hour playing him from inside the Turk, I told him it needed better ventilation, but was otherwise amenable.

The Dieppes live on the top floor of a building that overlooks the Seine and the rows of street salesmen that sell art, books, and other trinkets along the upper Left Bank. I decide to walk up beside the water, using my walking stick to navigate the uneven stones on the road. I feel as though I've overcompensated for my natural scent, which I've been told is quite powerful, by dousing myself in cologne. My hope is that the walk will somehow weaken the odor.

Mr. Dieppe works for the Bank of France in some impressive capacity; his wife is a minor actress, a woman whose beauty her children have clearly inherited. After their servant ushers me in, Mrs. Dieppe kisses me on both cheeks with a violence that nearly cripples. Her lips are swollen with color, her hair, compressed on top of her head, reminds me of an intricately decorated cabbage dyed the color of hay.

The house smells like oranges, with subtle hints of the incense that percolates during the sermons at Notre Dame. Thankfully, my smell is lost among competing odors.

"Ah, Master Augustine Kellp," Mr. Dieppe says, entering the hall with arms wide and bulging at the shirt's seams. He's tall and broad, an altar of symmetry, with a high forehead that has a curious tautness to it. He shakes my hand. "A wonderful display today," he says of Jacques's performance, leading me down the hall. My shoes clack on the wood. "I'm sad to have missed it. I understand you watched?"

"He was magnificent," I say, adding, "though undisciplined."

"Ah, yes, his great weakness." Mr. Dieppe claps me on the back and says that a bit of imperiousness isn't all that bad, all the time. He asks if the rumor's true, that I have a lady friend. "I won't tell, Kellp. What's spoken of between men stays between men, you know."

I make the requisite theatrics of denial, saying no no, I have no love, no paramour, though I secretly pine for his daughter. I made the mistake of leaving a poem I'd been drafting in her honor out during a lesson a few weeks ago with Jacques, who had found it, read it, and, evidently struck by its erotic content, mentioned it to his father who now mentions it to me, every time we meet. "Come, come, Kellp, there's no sense in denying yourself, even if you feel the need to deny her existence to me."

"Deny what?"

Clara materializes from another door, where we find ourselves now, in the living room, where a plate of sweet meats, cheeses, and bread has been set up in a circular table in the center. All around us, paintings from Germany, France, and elsewhere hang on the walls. When Clara takes her father's side she's a foot away from me. "Ah, Monsieur Kellp here has found himself a lady friend," Mr. Dieppe says.

"A what?" Clara's face becomes an explosion of loveliness, and I allow myself the fantasy that she's somehow jealous. "Is that true?"

Before I can answer, she bends over and takes my cheeks in her hands and presses her lips against my forehead.

"Don't be too touchy with him," Mr. Dieppe says, laughing. "You don't want to bugger it up for him. Imagine if word got back to her that he's got the affections of a younger woman. He'd never hear the end of it from his lady friend."

Clara is still holding my cheeks when she turns to him and says, "Daddy, please, don't embarrass him," and there's the vein in her neck again. When she finally lets go she says she has something to show me, before Jacques arrives, and brings me away from her father and to her room, a place I've never seen.

After showcasing the Turk in Schönbrunn Palace, Kempelen had been practically ordered to take a tour of Europe by the emperor, and so the two of us, or three—the Turk, for all its inhumanity, certainly did seem to have its own sort of life—traveled from court to court, via ship, carriage, and other locomotive measures. I, of course, traveled alone, under an itinerary set out by Kempelen; having us seen together aroused suspicion, and so I spent much of my time alone, reading, writing poetry (I was, and remain, a terrible poet, as my scribblings in Clara Dieppe's honor no doubt prove).

Around this time, Kempelen found himself longing for home, where he could stretch, instead of simply reiterate, his creative powers. In short: the Turk no longer held his interest. "It's a sham anyway," he said. We'd become something close to friends, though I detected more than a hint of disdain in the hours directly following any performance.

He wanted to focus on his other inventions, particularly the speaking machine, which he would display alongside the Turk, the latter acting as a kind of hook to engage interest in the former.

During that first marvellous evening, when I played for Joseph II, in the presence of Grand Duke Paul of Russia and Maria Feodorovna, the duchess, I defeated three opponents in one night. The duchess sat, aloof, next to her husband, who clapped as I trumped the attacks of the finest courtiers. Finally, he himself played, and proved inferior. I made sure to draw it out, to make the requisite sacrifices.

I had heard that the duchess was quite tall, certainly taller than the Turk. She had what might be called an impressive carriage, a backside that could, the rumors had it, support an entire three-course dinner upon it. I could imagine her sitting across the room, her legs, covered by the vast ruffles of her gown. On her feet, the slippers of the duke's previous wife, Natalia, as it was the duchess's habit to wear the clothes of her predecessor, despite the whispers that circulated about how quickly she did so.

Every so often, I would be distracted from my move by the thought of her foot's instep, the paleness of the cross hatching of veins there. (Yes, even then, I was intrigued by the veins of a woman; I was sure that the countess, like Clara Dieppe, was a geographical wonder of blood running through light purple tubes).

I made my moves from inside the Turk, pacing the game in the way Kempelen demanded, letting my opponent have the upper hand at least once in the match. It was a dull, unintellectual thrashing, comparable to the games I played with my father, from sick bed, in the days when my mother had left us and he was no doubt contemplating the hanging that took place a few days later.

I've been accused of having no feeling, no sense of empathy. Gallows humor. "You should've been an executioner," Kempelen said on a number of occasions, only to laugh when I corrected him by saying: "Oh, my dear sir, that's exactly what I am. An executioner. A killer limited in his homicides to the chess board."

Audience members often reported feeling an evil power, a demonic presence, emanating from the Turk. Since the Turk was an empty thing, mechanical but under my control, I must surmise that the audience members had been feeling me.

On our third night as guests of Joseph II, Maria Feodorovna ordered the Turk to be brought to her. Kempelen roused me from my hiding place in the room we shared and installed me within. "The countess wants to play the Turk," he said, half-naked and putting on his suit. I slithered into my hatch and into the cabinet, and in no time at all found the cabinet being transported through the palace halls.

I heard Kempelen and the attendants speak. When the cabinet started moving, Kempelen stayed behind. I could guess that his expression had grown grim, his eyes staring coldly in my direction.

"Ah," the countess said, once the Turk was stationed in the room. In my mind, she materialized from behind a set of veils, strategically positioned around the bed. I imagined she was wearing a robe, her hair flowing down her sides in a relaxed fashion.

Manipulating the mechanisms inside the Turk, I turned its head toward her and bowed slightly. She took black, I took white. She sat in a stool across from the Turk. Only the sound of her breathing could be heard over the metal on metal grinding of the gears near my torso and head.

She wasn't very good. We played one game, quite quickly, and she grew audibly upset when I cornered her king with a castle-and-rook checkmate. She insisted on setting the chessboard for a second game, and this one went for a bit longer. After she lost, she pulled open the doors of the cabinet to look inside. Here, she saw what all the crowds saw, when Kempelen opened them before a performance: a set of gears, mechanical implements, all phony.

When the third game passed, quicker than the first, she did something curious, and curiously haunting: she took the hand of the Turk and put it forcefully on her left breast. Though I could not see the Turk's hand upon her breast, the room was charged with such an energy that I am sure this is where she led the Turk's palm. She kept it there for a few seconds, breathing in deeply. Then she set it gently back on the chessboard, adjusted the bust of her dress, fabric sliding against skin, and asked that the Turk be taken away.

The countess stood, unmoving, as her attendants pushed the Turk through the door. Imagine standing at night and looking up at the moon and waiting for it to disintegrate into the bluish ether of the sky.

With the Turk safely installed in our quarters, Kempelen threw open the hatch. I practically spilled out, nearly suffocated.

He helped me out. "What the hell happened, Kellp?"

I needed a minute to catch my breath.

We both looked at the Turk. A strange smile seemed to have now appeared on his face.

———

Clara walks me by arm to her room, and I'm overcome by how unlike its owner it is. Clearly, someone else has decorated it; there is nothing to suggest the lived-in quality that I would expect. Everything is in its place. Her clothes are the clothes of any other person, piled neatly on a dresser. Her books are arranged by spine color and size, and on closer inspection I realize that somehow one book also shares with its two mates on either side similarity of theme, topic, or genre of literature. There is poetry, books on etiquette, religious texts. There is a Bible next to the bed.

I scan the room for any kind of life and I'm left only with Clara Dieppe, red in the cheeks, closing the door behind us, and an insane part of me believes (hopes, considers foisting the bible skyward and shouting a banshee's prayer) that Clara will see some of the handsome Turk in me. It's only a thought, and it dies quickly, the way most passion in my life has.

"You've been very good to my brother," she says.

"That's part of my job."

All at once she sits on the bed and sighs. I ask what's the matter.

"They're going to fire you. I tried to tell them not to. But they want to hire a more famous tutor for him."

I excuse myself to the water chamber and do nothing but stand and wonder and pick at a small tear in the wallpaper, near the wall at the doorframe. The rip grows larger as I pick, though in terms of vengeance, it's far from satisfying.

The day Kempelen and I were supposed to leave Shönbrunn Palace and the company of Maria Feodorovna, I wrote a poem from the Turk to the countess, intending to give it to her, to confess everything. I'd never told a woman I had loved her before; in fact, the Turk's touching of her chest had been the most intimate moment I'd had with a woman up to that point.

Kempelen found the poem and I was duly chastised. "Have you lost all your faculties, Kellp?" he shouted when we were away from prying eyes and ears. He held the poem up over my head like the canted blade of a guillotine.

He slapped me across the face. And slapped me again, and soon I couldn't feel my face any more. Tearing up the poem, he said, "If you ever try something stupid like this again, Kellp, I'll ruin you."

And so, here I am, picking at wallpaper, and thinking the same thought I've thought for fifty years. Kempelen is long dead. I am close to death myself. The countess, also dead. The Turk, though he hasn't been destroyed by time, is at the very least a rotting, gangrenous appendage affixed to me, a cancer of the memory.

Jacques Dieppe will be my last student. Clara Dieppe my last love. We tend to assume that things are meaningful, yet fail to grasp the meaning of those things until time has eroded them until non-essence. This, then, is the challenge of the living: to recognize the significance of the present.

Should I have confessed my love for the countess?

The Kellp of the past had decided no, that it wouldn't have made a speck of difference. She could never love me. She loved the Turk and, besides that, she was a countess and married, and I was a thumb of a man with a face that looked vaguely like the wrinkled skin of your elbow.

The Kellp of the present recognizes that yes, all of these things are true. But life isn't always about getting what one wants, nor is it about simply accepting one's lot as water accepts a rut in the bedrock.

Effort, however futile, is blood not yet cooled. Action is circulation. And what's bravery if not a refusal to accept one's fate?

Historically, I've never been much of a drinker. I am not a large man; my physiology has trouble with vices. So with Kempelen, it was chess, reading, poetry, less a double life as my own life gradually fusing to the Turk's, as the epiphyseal plates of the skull become imperceptible from one another, save for the thin knitting of bone.

At the dinner table of the Dieppes, a brocade of cheering, to Jacques's success in the chess tournament. The Dieppe Seniors toast me several times; Jacques gets drunk and so do I. Even Mrs. Dieppe seems to enjoy herself, the carafe of wine in front of her gradually imbibed.

Only Clara seems sullen, the pout of her lip noted only by myself and her father, who at one point says, "What's a matter with you?"

"Nothing's the matter," she says, picking at her omelette. A piece of egg crust sits on her lip and I want to pick it off.

I'm drunk. I have reconciled myself to some sort of extreme action. Our conversation borders on inane prattle. Mr. Dieppe asks me how I feel about T__, a recently retired chess master.

"Not entirely terrible," I respond, honestly. "I've seen him play. Never played the man myself."

Mr. Dieppe nods, rubs his face. Not for the first time, it occurs to me that there is a touch of entitlement in Mr. Dieppe's eyes, like a spider who's inherited the web of another and expects it to feed him night and day. In fact, Dieppe's position in the bank comes as a result of old money.

Taking the rest of the wine in my glass, I ask if T__ is to be my replacement. Dieppe's face drops.

"Your replacement, Mr. Kellp?"

I sweep my hand to Jacques, nearly knocking over Mrs. Dieppe's carafe. "Your son. Is this chess master meant to replace me?"

Jacques, who has been in conversation with his mother at my left, has stopped talking. He looks at his father, who takes the napkin off his lap and sets it down on the table. "Well, we were going to wait until after dinner to go into business matters."

"Why not now?" I say, emboldened by the wine and by the way Clara looks at me from across the table. This isn't love, the illumination coming from her more the stuff of flame than the moon, but it's enough.

Jacques clears his throat. Mrs. Dieppe clears her throat.

"There will be a severance," Dieppe says. "A very generous one."

"I had no idea," Jacques says, "I swear," and even he has trouble believing his own words.

Mrs. Dieppe, attuned to the delicate balance that has developed, stands and asks Clara to join her in the living room. I tell her to sit. I do so with such force and realize the inappropriateness of my timbre.

"Pardon me?" Mrs. Dieppe says.

"I wasn't speaking to you, madame. I was speaking to your daughter."

Clara sits and, in a gesture I've seen only a few times since knowing her, bites the flesh of her index finger.

"Mr. Kellp," Dieppe says, "I think you're out of line. What we're speaking about is business, among men. You have proved a satisfactory tutor for my son, and I believe I have been more than generous in my thanks. But he's progressed to a level where he needs someone more established."

"I can charge you more," I say, not altogether joking, "if it would please you."

In my drunken state, I address Clara and explain that she is beautiful and that I'm in love with her. I tell Jacques that, at best, he will be a middling chess player, that he lacks the intellect, foresight, and self-discipline to achieve any success worth discussing. To Mrs. Dieppe I say that her facepaint makes her look like a trollop, and for Mr. Dieppe, I save the condemnation last used on Kempelen himself, the day he discharged me, remembering Erasmus as best I can: *In a world of the blind, those with one eye will come to rule.*

Outside, in the warm air, I feel nauseous, old, heavy in the liver. At home, I replay the game I had with Philidor on a worn chessboard. Since Kempelen died and the Turk was sold to a Frenchman, it has played and defeated the likes of Emperor Napoleon himself. Thinking of this, I wonder how many souls the Turk will have before its death, and what a shame it is that I've sold mine to a machine.

Someone Else

Diana Xin
University of Montana; MFA

And the zombie said, "Where is my head?"
— *Elizabeth Oliva*

The day Holly and Sean moved into their first home together, they found a dead animal lying along the wooden slats of their back deck. It was unclear what kind of animal. The head was gone. There was something that looked like a nose, or a snout, and maybe half an ear, but no head. Clumps of gray and brown fur stuck to the boot-length mass of blood and flesh and entrails. Flies dotted portions of the corpse where bits of bone showed through. It was a fresh kill.

"This is not good," Holly said. "This is a bad omen."

"Don't be ridiculous," Sean said. "This is nature."

He stood over the carcass (of a raccoon? a possum? what?), holding a shovel he had found in the shed. He would have to pick up the carcass with the shovel and take it down the connecting stairs into the yard because they were on the second floor. And then what? Bury it in a hole? Dump it in the garbage can? They had no plastic bags. Everything was packed away.

"Don't bury it here," Holly said. "I want it gone. Take it away. Would you? Please?"

"How? I'm not walking down the street with it."

"I don't know. I can't look at it anymore. I'm going to be sick if I keep looking at it."

She went back inside to unpack. After unloading a box of dishes, she looked out the glass panes of the door. Sean was digging a hole near the far end of the chain link fence.

"Is it gone?" she asked him when he came back in.

"Yes," he said, running his hands under the faucet. "I took care of it."

Holly paused with a salad bowl in her hand, but she didn't ask any questions. She didn't want to make him lie.

Holly and Sean met in college in Evanston, when they both lived in Shepard Hall. Holly was a performance studies major, and Sean was doubling in economics and English. It had made him seem very well balanced. Numbers and words. Now he had a job in numbers that allowed him to work from home, where he spent half his hours struggling with words. He had a screenplay inside of him. He was coaxing it out with whiskey and a typewriter. Slowly. She was a barista-bartender at the Heartland Café in Rogers Park. Between her shifts, she memorized scripts and acted out small parts in local Chicago theaters. She had played a blind painter, a Victorian maid, a snail who committed suicide. These were her specs: Caucasian, 5'10", brunette, long hair, slim build, tattoo of a hummingbird above her right hipbone. The back of her headshot listed the following skills: yoga, tap dance, juggling, bird impressions, good with animals and children.

After Holly's roommate moved back to Michigan, she and Sean counted up the time and concluded that they had been dating for, give and take, almost four years, if they skipped the break-ups. Four years seemed like enough time. Sean did the numbers thing. They would each save three hundred fifty dollars a month. It was a decision that made itself, a no-brainer.

They chose Andersonville. They could afford it, and it was a move in the right direction. Everyone from the north moved south, neighborhood by neighborhood until they reached the Gold Coast. Then they stopped, or returned to the suburbs. In Andersonville, they were near three independent theaters, as well as the Swedish Bakery, the Hopleaf, and the dilapidated Taste of Lebanon that served the best lentil soup, for only two dollars.

They found a place three blocks from Clark Street, going away from the lake; the upstairs level of a two-story. It was bigger than what they envisioned, but cheap. They would still save two hundred thirty dollars a month.

"Best deal in town," the landlord had said. "Can't find another place like it. Hardwood floors everywhere. Look at these windows. Look at these countertops. Imagine slicing tomatoes on these countertops."

The countertops were black and marbled. The landlord was short and hairy. He'd worn dark sunglasses indoors, even though it was cloudy out. He assured them that the neighborhood was great, the laundry was free, parking was easy, and they would save money.

"That kitchen itself is worth its weight in gold," he said. "You'll like cooking in it so much you won't *want* to eat out. And downstairs is empty right now, so really, you'll be getting the whole house."

"Can we use the downstairs area, too?" Sean asked.

"Well, no. I'd have to give you the key."

"Can we see the downstairs?" Holly asked.

"No. I'm still fixing it up."

He was a strange man, but the unit was lovely. High ceilings lifted up over the expansive living room, and a large bay window looked out onto the quiet street. Summerdale Avenue had a nice ring, and it was lush with trees. They could fit a small dining table by the bay window, and still arrange the couch and bookcases around the stone fireplace. A narrow hallway led from the living room past the bathroom and the bedroom, into the kitchen and a small sunroom where Sean could set up office. A door in the kitchen led out to the deck, which then led downstairs into the yard. Holly imagined planting flowers and herbs, growing her own mint and basil, even though their lease began August 1, past planting season.

But now that they had their own things inside of it, the place felt less inviting, less like home. They tried rearranging the furniture, a difficult feat with half-emptied boxes all over the place. They'd push all the boxes to one side of the room and move the couch along the wall or to the middle of the room at an angle matching the fireplace. A few days later, they would do it again, returning the couch to its original place against the inside wall. Then they'd move the armchair and the coffee table and the bookcase and the floor lamp. The boxes always got in the way.

Sean found a painting of a nude woman sitting between two trees at the Brown Elephant thrift store. He made Holly close her eyes before he unveiled it. "Isn't it cool?" he said. "It looks like a Dalí or one of those paintings where the man's face is an apple."

The woman sat cross-legged on a stone block between the trees, meditating with her back to the viewer, like she was looking into the painting rather than out at the world. The block was etched with two mountains shaped like lips. Above her, two leaves drooping from the trees made slanted, emerald eyes. The woman herself was shaped like a nose, the top of her legs flaring out into nostrils. Beneath all this, an incomprehensible plate of fruit.

"Do you see it?" Sean asked. "Do you see the face? Isn't that neat?"

It felt played out to Holly, but Sean's excitement was always so genuine and uninhibited that she could never say no, so she helped him hang it up over the fireplace.

"That's what we need," Sean said. "More art on the walls."

"I think we just need time. And we need to unpack."

She picked her way back through the obstacle course of boxes and sat down at the table. It was becoming a situation, their boxes. She could never find anything she needed. Whenever she thought she'd put something away, it would show up somewhere else, or back inside a box. Perhaps three weeks was not enough time to get settled, but they should at least have unpacked all their things.

Sean beamed proudly at his painting. "I think it'll make us more peaceful," he said.

But Holly could no longer see the meditating woman, only the tilting green leaf eyes, mocking and mysterious.

When Holly woke in the middle of the night, she could have sworn that someone had called her name. But Sean was asleep. Sean was a very serious sleeper, his face always contorted in concentration. He never looked peaceful or relaxed. Mildly tortured, maybe. The childish tuck of his hand underneath his cheek was a strange contradiction.

She settled back in and tried to find comfort in the warmth of his back and the rhythm of his snores, but her heart was frantic. Not because of a nightmare. She couldn't remember any dreams. It felt like something or someone desperately needed her attention, but she was desperately ignoring it. Like some horrible realization was getting ready to break out in a rash of hives on her skin. The ceiling fan whirred its smooth circles above her, the blades blurring into invisibility like insect wings. Holly grew hot so she kicked off the covers. Sean grunted in his sleep. She watched the fan spin until morning.

She felt more like herself again at work, taking orders for eggs and pancakes and sandwiches. The regulars came in, ordering the same food and telling the same jokes. *Do you know what they call a Quarter Pounder with cheese in France?* And she'd shake her head, no.

But when it was time to go home, her chest began to constrict again. Drops of rain stung her face. She walked hunched against the wind, which was quickly blowing the summer away. It was not that she didn't enjoy living with Sean. She loved Sean. It was the house she didn't like. There was something wrong about it, but she didn't know what. The whole atmosphere changed in density when she entered the front doors, the mustiness growing heavier and thicker as she trudged up the stairs. The door to their unit was not entirely closed. She pushed it open and found another woman sitting inside, a girl with white-blonde hair.

"Oh," she said, stopping at the doorway. "Hello."

For a moment, she thought she had walked into the wrong home. She had taken a turn too early, gone up a different flight of stairs. She flinched with embarrassment and almost apologized as the girl turned to look at her, cocking her head with curiosity. A can of beer dangled from her hand. She was holding it from above, her arm tossed over the edge of the purple armchair. Holly's purple armchair. This *was* her home. She recognized her things. As if to confirm it, Sean came walking down the hallway, a bottle of Jameson in his hand.

"You're home," he said. "Let me get you a glass."

"I'm Juliet," the girl said, rising now. "You must be Holly. I've heard so much about you."

Holly squinted at her, but she couldn't place her, even though she had a very distinctive, pixie face, and that white-blonde hair. "I'm sorry. Have we met?"

"I'm your new neighbor." The girl moved closer as if to hug her. Holly crossed her arms to fend it off.

"My fiancée and I just moved in downstairs," Juliet went on. "But George went to work today, and I had to supervise the movers. They moved the furniture but left all the boxes on the street. Thank God Sean was here. He's so nice."

Sean came back and poured whiskey into three tumblers. "Did you know that Juliet here is a filmmaker?" he said. "Isn't that terrific?" He gave Holly a meaningful look before continuing. "She acts, too. On-camera work. What are the chances, right? That she moves in right below us?"

He was already a little drunk. Holly could tell. He pulled over a chair from the small dining table and sat straddling the seatback. "So you were saying about that new project?"

Holly crossed her legs on the couch. She tried to follow along, but her attention seemed unnecessary, and the whiskey overwhelmed her sleep-groggy head. She allowed her eyes to grow heavy, until Juliet exclaimed, "We would love to join you for dinner. Thank you so much."

Holly fixed her eyes on Sean, but he was looking at Juliet.

"Let me call George and tell him to come upstairs when he gets home," she said.

Finally, Holly caught Sean's eyes, and tried to convey her displeasure. He only shrugged. "Don't worry about it. We're just being good neighbors."

So Holly went to the kitchen and began preparing a chicken cacciatore. Sean and Juliet came along to help, but really they just stood in the way, talking about some film set in Salem, or a Blair Witch Project deal.

"So what's your dream role? If you could play any role in the world?" Sean was asking Juliet, who tilted her head thoughtfully, dramatically.

She leaned forward and widened her eyes before she spoke. Holly could recognize a scene being set. She saw it all the time, among actors. "I want one of those roles in a horror film. The girl pursued by demons."

Holly studied Juliet's angular frame and pasty skin. She could see a compatibility there. Juliet had the horror film look of a possessed child, or a bleached scarecrow. She handed Sean the lettuce. "Help me make a salad."

It turned out all right, after the chicken was set to stew, and Sean had assembled the salad and opened some chilled wine. Energized by the cooking, Holly could sit down and feign interest in Juliet. "Where are you from? How long have you been in the city?"

She was from Ohio and had moved here eight years ago, right after she dropped out of college at twenty-one. Holly was surprised. She had seemed younger, but perhaps she was just smaller. Some people were simply built like children, Holly supposed, but really they weren't. Juliet was telling another story, about the last gig she had signed up for but never completed because the director had leered at her during the nude scenes, and made an unsavory proposal. She was just about to say what the proposal was, when there was a knock on the door.

"That must be George," Juliet said.

Holly opened the door. "Hello, welcome—"

George blinked at her from behind his thick-framed black glasses. "Holly," he said. "What are you doing here?"

"George," Holly said, before turning back to the others. "Sean, George is here."

During the junior year break-up, Holly had spent many hours sitting across from George's owlish, blinking eyes. They had met in Calculus. She was failing, for the second time, and George offered to help. Sad that Sean had called it quits, she accepted eagerly, and only partly because of George's poorly hidden crush. When Sean 180'd back to her, she had actually hesitated about leaving George and his gentle, diffident ways, enough so that the brief, four-month relationship became a sore point for Sean. "I can't believe you slept with that guy," he would say, every once in a while, out of nowhere.

"George." Sean rose from his chair. "So you're George. I knew you were George. *A* George." A faint blush came creeping up his neck.

"This is my fiancé," Juliet announced.

"We're so happy you're here," Holly said.

George blinked. "I brought a lemon roll."

"Wonderful."

Holly refilled her glass and got another one for George. It was not implausible for George to move in below them. Many of their classmates were now scattered throughout Chicago. Still, what were the chances? She left the others to puzzle this out as she busied herself serving the chicken.

They ate around the table by the bay window, crowded too close together. The meal opened in awkward silence. Only Juliet seemed free of it, delighted, in fact, by the coincidence that they had all known each other. "But not very well," Sean clarified. He and George talked in tentative tones, each figuring out what the other had been up to since the major intersection of their lives three years ago, figuring out who had been more successful. George was working as a data analyst at a large bank downtown. Holly was uncertain if this caused Sean to envy or pity him. She sighed, thinking how men were just like dogs, sniffing each other's assholes to decide who was alpha.

"This chicken is delicious," George said.

"I'm glad you like it." Holly smiled at the memory of his soft-spoken compliments, his small kindnesses. She smiled at the way his dark, almost black, hair still fell across the side of his face, over the edge of the thick-framed glasses. Back then he had encouraged her to pursue a fledgling interest in developmental psychology and early childhood education, wooing her with his fervent praise of financial stability and Roth IRAs and career assessment. He had an ingrained practicality, borne from his middle-class, Midwestern upbringing. Sean had none of that, and found it exciting that she was an artist. Another sign that had confirmed her decision—a week after Sean asked to get back together, she got a lead role in the annual musical production. With the rehearsal schedule, she had to drop psychology.

   She felt Sean's eyes from across the table. He looked at her coldly, with a pouting jut of the chin that meant she had hurt his feelings. She had revealed too much, somehow, in the look on her face, even though she wasn't even sure what it was, exactly, that he had seen. She tried to think of a way to apologize, but Juliet began to talk again—did she ever stop?—and Sean turned away.

"I'll write a movie for you," he declared. "Yeah. Let's do a project together."

"Will you?" Juliet clasped her hands together and held them beneath her chin.

The gesture was so childish Holly struggled to reconcile the fact that Juliet was the oldest one in the room. She couldn't help but raise an eyebrow at George. This was where his practicality had led him? He shrugged. Sheepish, it seemed. At least Juliet had chosen him. Holly looked down at her plate, ashamed.

Sean still refused to meet her gaze, even as they began to clear and stack the plates. Frustrated anger brought tears to her eyes. After all, he was the one who had brought this onto them, inviting strangers over to dinner. She took this out on the plates, banging them one after the other into the dishwasher.

Back in the living room, Sean and Juliet sat on the couch, faces lit up by the screen of Sean's laptop. They were discussing his writing, which he guarded passionately from Holly. George sat in the purple armchair, looking sardonic as he sipped his wine. "They're going to make a movie," he said to Holly.

"What's it about?"

"Who the hell knows?"

Holly decided she wanted these people out of her home. The quickest way was to serve dessert. George came to help, watching her lay out new plates for the lemon roll.

"So how did you meet Juliet?" What she really wanted to know was how they had come to be engaged.

"Friend introduced us," George said. "About two years ago. Not a very long time, but you know."

"So when's the wedding?"

"Soon, probably. Juliet's not getting any younger. We haven't figured out anything for sure."

"Well, congratulations. She's very lucky."

"And you're still with Sean, I see."

Something about the way he said it alerted Holly to a new, snide and sneaking cruelty within George. Juliet's influence, probably. She looked over at Sean, hunched over his computer and handing sheaths of his hard work over to Juliet. He hid his eager hopes with self-deprecating comments and unquestioning deference. Holly's heart swelled for him.

She kept her voice light when she turned back to George. "He's the best. It's been so great, getting to live together."

Later that night, she wanted to tell Sean how she had stood up for him, how he was, without a doubt, the better man. But a rift had come between them, and she could only stand on the other side of it, watching and feeling his presence but unable to touch him. They did not kiss or even wish each other good night.

"How strange for them to move in *here*," Holly said.

"Juliet was nice," Sean replied, after a pause.

She fell asleep quickly, exhausted from the night before, but her dreams were vivid and disturbing. The animal buried in the corner of the yard crept in through the window, headless and shapeless, a mass of rotting flesh plagued by flies and their quivering larvae. All night, the animal-beast trod inside her mind, and when she woke at morning she was sluggish and bad tempered, not at all refreshed.

What did Holly love about Sean? Well, for starters, many things. On their second date, Holly had left her wallet at Clarke's Diner, and they abandoned a movie right before an exciting confrontation to go in search of it. Sean found it underneath one of the red vinyl benches. She apologized effusively, but he shrugged and said, "I was kind of hoping for a milkshake anyway." Perhaps it was because the last guy had been so short tempered, had taken every opportunity to foist an alcoholic beverage on her, but the milkshake seemed significant. Another time,

Holly was burning up with fever, and Sean called the student health center to demand that they stop testing her for strep but offer actual medical advice. Later, when they knew each other well enough to fight, he once said, mid-argument, "Even though you make me want to put my head through a wall, I still *care* about you." It was the sweetest thing a man had ever said to her, and far more moving and convincing than George's timorous declarations of love.

She tried to remember these things when she returned home and found Juliet on the armchair or the couch, or hidden back in Sean's office, peering over at the text he was typing. At least three times a week, Juliet would come upstairs in the afternoon and they would work on the script together until evening. Holly could smell it when Juliet was there. She brought a strange odor with her, a saccharine redolence that didn't quite hide the stench of something else beneath. She smelled like overripe flowers beginning to rot. When she came, Holly would read a book in the living room, or knit, or look through casting calls, though she hadn't felt inspired to audition for a long time. Most often, she would end up studying the painting that was supposed to make them peaceful, watching it shift from meditating woman to shady leaf-eyes back to woman then back to eyes. When all the disparate objects, and the spaces between them, connected into a face of sky and desert, and the face grew large enough to loom out of the painting, the eyes would remain, sometimes mournful, sometimes condemning.

George did not usually join them for these evenings. Juliet said his work was very demanding. When he did come up, it was with the express purpose of fetching his fiancé, but Juliet would take her time directing Sean on what to cut and what to tweak, so Holly was forced to make small talk with George, while enduring Sean's sullen looks.

One night after finishing up, Juliet demanded a glass of wine. "Or whiskey, or gin, or something."

Apparently, real strides had been made, and they could begin thinking about production.

"A toast," George said, raising his glass. "To the next Oscar-winning partnership."

Holly did not approve of his new sarcasm. It went against his personality, and he wasn't very good at it.

Despite the celebratory occasion, they all drank quietly, somberly.

"Do you know? I think this place is haunted." Juliet said this thoughtfully, looking up at the ceiling. There was nothing dramatic or affected, so Holly knew that she meant it.

George groaned. "This again?"

"I'm serious." Juliet turned to George. "How do you explain the spoons?"

"What are the spoons?" Sean asked.

Juliet explained that after she had come home from an advertising gig a few days before, she found all of their spoons lined up in a row along the countertop. George had not done it, and she certainly hadn't. Yet there they were, the spoons all in a row.

Holly felt a chill. Above the fireplace, the slanting leaf eyes seemed to turn to her, their serrated lashes accusatory. But what had she done? She had touched no spoons.

"We need to talk to the landlord," George said. "Someone must have our key. Do you know who lived here, before us?"

"No one," Holly said. "The unit was empty."

"There were claw marks on the wall, too," Juliet said. "Behind the front door. Three long claw marks."

Holly thought of the animal in the back yard, trying to remember if they had seen any limbs, anything with claws.

"I'm sure that was always there," George said. "We just missed it on the walk-through."

Sean clutched the stem of his glass with a tight fist. "That landlord. I knew he couldn't be trusted. He was way too short."

They fell back into silence, but now it was heavy and antagonistic.

"Are your counters marbled too?" Sean asked.

George and Juliet looked at him.

"The landlord was very proud of our countertops," Holly explained.

Juliet sighed. "I wish we could stay up here. It feels safer here."

Holly shook her head. "We're haunted, too."

After they left, at George's insistence that he needed to get to bed, Holly turned to Sean. "What if we're haunted?"

"You heard George," Sean said. "It's the landlord. I knew he was shady. I had a read on him."

Holly brought the glasses to the sink. As she washed them, she couldn't help but feel like she was being watched. She often felt this way now, because of the leaf-eyes hanging above the fireplace. But now she was in the kitchen, and she could still feel those eyes. She turned off the faucet, and looked around the empty kitchen. She checked the spoons. They lay nestled in the drawer, unremarkable. Sean was in his office, the typewriter clacking away. Holly pressed her fingers to the glass pane on the deck door. She could see nothing, with the light in the kitchen lighting up the darkness outside. Anything could be out there. That was the theorem of being inside. When you were inside, anything could be outside. She wondered if the woman in the painting felt the same. She wondered if the woman was really looking inside, or actually outside, or if it was all the same.

She checked the lock on the door and walked over to Sean's office. He looked up at her expectantly, silently asking what she wanted.

"Well, how's it going?" she said. "Do you like the script?"

"It's going all right. I think I'm getting somewhere."

"So it's about a girl who was cursed by her grandmother?"

"She inherits the curse," Sean explained. "Her grandmother makes a pact with a demon, but breaks it, so the curse goes to her."

"I suppose Juliet is going to play her?"

"That was the plan. But I think she's going to focus on directing."

"Oh."

"And I never really saw her for the role," Sean continued. "I was writing it for her, supposedly, but I think I wrote it for you."

"Oh," Holly said again, at an altogether different note.

"So—would you?"

"I would love to."

And that seemed to dissipate all the unhappiness that had simmered the past few weeks.

It stormed all morning the day they scheduled to shoot, but the sky cleared up by the afternoon, when they began. Juliet brought an assistant, a red-haired, freckled woman with braces. She was very mousy, and the metal over her teeth seemed to give her smile an unnatural stretch.

"What pretty skin. What a pretty nose. How pretty," she murmured as she did Holly's makeup. Holly had said she could do it herself, but Juliet insisted that Renee was the best.

"And we want you to get the star treatment," Juliet said.

Holly sat reviewing her lines as Juliet and Sean discussed the set and then began to rearrange the furniture. Holly took a deep breath, hoping they would remember the exact angle of where everything had been. She had just begun to feel comfortable inside her home. Juliet brought a few props as well, setting them around the room. They were tacky, thrift store items, meant to look like Wiccan talismans or something. A giant, brass pentagon star, an astrological chart, a silver goblet, and a metal skull. Juliet lit some candles and incense. A heady, sticky scent filled the room, but even that was not enough to cover up Juliet's odor of decay, which seemed to be growing stronger, Holly thought.

George came up to watch as well. He still walked the same way, shoulders tight with hands tucked into his pockets, but that used to be from shyness and now it was from pride, from wanting to keep himself separate from any kind of foolishness. Holly refused to play the small talk game with him, focusing instead on Sean's script. She had never read his work before. Seeing his words was like accessing some part of him she had never known. She tried to be respectful of it.

She had a question about character motivation and objective, and went to the kitchen where Juliet and Sean were conferencing. Still hidden in the hallway, she saw the two of them standing by the black marbled counters. Juliet had her hand on Sean's cheek. Even as the bad feeling rushed over her, Holly thought, maybe it's just nothing, but still her stomach twisted and her thoughts jumped to all the possible scenarios that could unfold. Sean would leave her, and Juliet would move in upstairs, just like she wanted. Holly did not think of what would become of herself, but only of Sean. Juliet would not stick around. She was much too flaky. Two years tops and she would be gone. What would happen if Sean got sick? Not with cold or flu, but something horrible and immutable. Something that caused blood in the bowels. Who would take care of him? The thought of it brought tears to Holly's eyes. Her throat tightened. Couldn't he understand how much she loved him?

She rushed into the bathroom before they could see her and washed her hands and face, forgetting her makeup, which was ruined. Renee clucked her tongue over the braced teeth and cleaned off the smeared mascara before reapplying everything. "What pretty skin," she said again. "What pretty eyebrows." Her fingertips were rough like paper as they brushed across Holly's cheeks. George peered up at her from his magazine occasionally, but continued flipping the pages with rhythmic regularity. He was reading *The Economist*. Nothing frivolous for George.

And then they were ready. Juliet set up the lights and Renee held the reflector. Holly assumed position by the fireplace, ready to say her lines. She did not look angry. She did not look crestfallen. She knew how to get into character. She could shed the old Holly, forget all the troubles and uncertainties, become Holly-in-Anastasia, the ridiculous name Sean had given his non-Slavic heroine.

Juliet called action and Holly tried to make the last shift into someone else, but there were no curtains rising, no stage lights blinding her from the gaze of the rustling audience. Sean smiled at her broadly, arms crossed in front of his chest. George paused in the middle of a page turn to arch an eyebrow. Renee's oblong smile glinted from the corner of the room.

"Is there a problem?" Juliet asked. Her eyes were and black and intent inside her pallid face.

"I'm sorry," Holly said. "Can we start over?"

She made it through the stage directions in the first scene. The prescriptive looks of wonder and bewilderment were easy given her current state, but she spoke the lines haltingly, talking to the air. "Yes . . . yes . . . I'd like to report an incident. . . . No, this was my grandmother's house. But she's dead now. . . . There are dead things here." Whose words were these? Did they belong to her or Sean or Juliet? Or to someone else entirely?

They did three more takes, with Juliet requesting small adjustments in the way she brushed back her hair, where she stood when she made the scripted phone call.

"It would be easier," she said, "if there were someone else in the scene."

"Maybe," George said, "you should consider the psychology of your character."

Holly narrowed her eyes at him, who wasn't even a part of anything. Juliet pulled Sean back to the kitchen, to have another conference. Holly peered down the long, dim hallway, but could not even see their shadows. She pictured Juliet kissing Sean, contaminating his face with her hot, putrid breath, her stringy saliva. She imagined all of her caked on make-up, her bloodless skin peeling off in one layer to reveal the festering rot underneath, twitching flesh decomposing off the bone. Holly's stomach turned over.

"I wonder what they're talking about," she said.

George shrugged.

"Does it ever bother you? That Juliet maintains such close relationships with other men?"

"Juliet is Juliet. It's no use trying to change her."

"And you're happy with her, the way she is?"

"It is what it is," he said, and then he turned back to his magazine, flipping another page.

Holly raised her eyes to the leaf-eyes in the painting. Between their shade, the woman bowed her head. Finally, Holly understood that the woman was not meditating, but praying, and the plate of fruit was her offering. She was not looking out at the sky and the desert, but the sky and the desert were rushing to meet her, to carry her away. And now the eyes faded back into leaves, and Holly thought of the empty space between the trees, how it could take on its own solidity, how the trees would still frame that space even in the woman's absence.

"Well, let's try this again." Juliet's voice floated down from the hallway.

Holly turned, watching as Juliet and Sean emerged from the darkness, their pale, blond bodies moving as one. Juliet's beady black eyes were sharp and soulless. How had Holly not noticed this before?

Holly turned back to the painting. The woman seemed to speak to her, inside her mind, promising her freedom and possibility. She was not a woman trapped in the pose of meditation, but a woman for whom the whole world was opening up. The leaves seemed to nod to her, encouraging.

"Ready for another go?" Sean asked, reaching a hand out to her.

Holly backed away. She backed into the front door and reached behind her to twist the knob. The click of the lock as the door sprung open resounded inside her body. A rush of air swept over her, so clean without the hazy incense and syrupy rot. This was the final push she needed, to cross the line out of her life.

"Where are you going?" Sean said.

Holly turned from him, racing down the stairs, through the front doors and into the fresh, rain-washed streets.

"Wait," Sean called out behind her. "Come back."

But she was running free. She was not looking back. The wind picked up the ends of her hair and she was sailing away, racing toward this other person that she knew she could be.

Printed by Libri Plureos GmbH in Hamburg, Germany